Riptide

Also by Debbi Mack

Least Wanted

Identity Crisis

Five Uneasy Pieces

Riptide

Debbi Mack

Renegade Press
Savage, MD

Renegade Press
P.O. Box 156
Savage, MD

This is a work of fiction. Any resemblance to actual events or persons, living or dead, is entirely coincidental.

Library of Congress Cataloging-in-Publication Data
Riptide by Debbi Mack
ISBN: 978-0-9829508-5-2
Library of Congress Control Number: 2011963214

DEDICATION

For Joyce and Andrew Mack, my parents, two of the most stubborn individuals and, in their own way, the best role models I could ever have.

For Rick Iacangelo, my husband, who's stood beside this stubborn individual at the best and worst of times and always believed in me.

ACKNOWLEDGMENTS

As I write this, I think about the essentially impossible task of thanking everyone who's ever helped me. The writing community is a highly supportive one, and I feel truly grateful to have been helped by many people along the way. My current writers' group has contributed so much, in terms of suggestions, constructive criticism, and overall support, that I want to thank all the members (past and present), including Janet Benrey, Ray Flynt, Sasscer Hill, Mary Ellen Hughes, Trish Marshall, Sherriell Mattingley, Bonnie Settle, Thomas Sprenkle, Marcia Talley, and Lyn Taylor. All of you have been an invaluable aid to my growth as a writer. I also owe a great debt of gratitude to Pat Altner, Jack Bludis, Carla Buckley, Carolyn Males, Ellen Rawlings, Louise Titchener, and other writers and friends who provided helpful suggestions and encouragement along the way.

With respect to this book, I'd like to thank the public information office of the Ocean City Police Department for answering questions about police procedure, jurisdiction and detention. The vast majority of my research on the poultry and crab industry, immigration issues, and race relations on the Eastern Shore was on the Internet, including online news, legislative, historical and other documentation. Some of the story is based on personal and anecdotal information. The rest, as they say, is just fiction. Any errors or omissions on these subjects are my own. My endless thanks to Peter Ratcliffe for providing the great cover art and Beth Rubin for her awesome editing. Many thanks also to my friends in the Chesapeake Chapter of Sisters in Crime, and to Laurie Cullen for copyediting and handling the formatting for this techno-idiot. Extra special thanks to Eileen Bernstein for reviewing the Spanish text for punctuation and syntax. Any of Sam's usage or grammatical errors are entirely her fault, of course.

JUNE 2006

CHAPTER ONE

The pounding woke me. I felt for the bedside lamp, turned it on, and looked around the unfamiliar room.

The swimsuit flung onto the broken wicker chair told me I was in the right place.

My best friend Jamila and I had rented the condo for a week, a gift to ourselves before pressing flesh at the annual bar association convention in Ocean City, Maryland. I usually bypassed the conference, along with Brussels sprouts and whiny kids, whenever possible. Jamila shamed me into going, since she was slated to speak. The topic was legal ethics. There wasn't a room at the convention center big enough to accommodate everyone who should have attended.

We had checked in on Saturday, aka "change day" in the world of beach rentals. Not that I'd know. This was my first vacation in forever.

I'd left my case files, my calendar, my briefcase, and my cares back in my office on Main Street in Laurel. My neighbor Russell was looking after my cat Oscar in my stead. Russell is like the gay father I never had. He's not a huge cat fan, but he's a great friend.

More pounding. The noise came from the front door. I glanced at the bedside clock. 1:35 A.M. *What the fuck?*

The banging resumed. I rolled out of bed, trudged to the door and opened it. Jamila stood in the short hall between our rooms. She held a creamy white bathrobe closed across her sizeable chest.

Jamila looked amazing for someone who'd been startled out of bed in the wee hours. Despite pillow-tousled hair and sleepy eyes, she was a dusky Queen of Sheba in figure-revealing silk to my anemic court jester in striped men's pajamas.

"Who on earth could that be, Sam?" Jamila hissed.

"I don't know." My words were stupid and obvious.

Another round of pounding. I moved to the door and peered through the peephole, before our visitor pounded his knuckles bloody.

On the other side stood a uniformed cop.

Sighing, I opened the door.

"Good evening, ma'am," the cop said.

"Good morning, you mean." *Wail on my door in the middle of the night and you're guaranteed an audience with the Wicked Witch of the West.*

The cop took a step back then recovered quickly.

"Sorry to wake you at this hour—" he started.

I cut him off. "Please tell me this doesn't have to do with our friends on the first floor. I thought we had that straightened out."

"No ma'am. This is far more serious."

It better be. And quit calling me ma'am.

I heard Jamila shuffle up behind me.

A female officer moved into view. She consulted a notepad. "Are you Stephanie Ann McRae?" she asked.

"Right. What's this about?"

The woman ignored me. "And you're Jamila Williams?"

"Yes." Jamila sounded tired, unsure. She moved closer.

"Is this yours, Ms. Williams?" The man held up a plastic bag containing a decorative tortoise shell comb. The four-pronged, fan-shaped comb was distinctively marbled.

Jamila blinked. "Can I see that?"

He handed it to her for inspection.

"It … looks like one of mine," she said. "One that I lost. Where did you find this?"

The cops exchanged a look.

"I'm sorry, ma'am, but you need to come with us."

"What?" I said. "What the hell is this?"

"Ms. Williams, we need to take you in for questioning."

Adrenaline pumped through me, bringing me to full alert. "Questioning?" My voice was shrill. "What's going on?"

"William Raymond Wesley has been murdered. We just need to ask you a few questions at the station."

The man droned on. The night had turned surreal. I tried to get more specifics, but Jamila silenced me with a raised hand. Probably didn't want to look uncooperative. Reluctantly, I backed down.

Everyone seemed to move in slow motion. The woman escorted Jamila to her room so she could get dressed.

Who the hell is William Raymond Wesley?

Then, I remembered.

Jamila emerged in a warm-up suit. With a firm hand on Jamila's arm, the female cop escorted her while holding onto an evidence bag with her pajamas and robe. Jamila and I exchanged a look that said she, too, recalled how we'd met the victim.

CHAPTER TWO

Jamila and I had gone shopping for antiques on Sunday. Which is to say, Jamila wanted to shop for antiques and I dragged my ass along.

We took a spin to a small shop outside Berlin, Maryland. A mom-and-pop outfit in the middle of nowhere. Inside the store, Jamila took her time browsing while I stifled yawns.

A lacquered rosewood music box caught Jamila's eye.

"Isn't that pretty?" she asked.

I made approving noises. I had to admit, the image of kittens on the box was cute. However, I hate knickknacks. More stuff to gather dust and cat hair.

After checking the price, Jamila made a counter offer. The saleswoman may have looked like Aunt Bee on *The Andy Griffith Show*, but she drove a hard bargain.

Having reached a happy compromise, the lady wrapped Jamila's new treasure and placed it in a gift box.

"You all have a lovely day, girls," she said, beaming as if life couldn't get better.

I followed Jamila to her silver Beemer. The spring in her step matched the saleslady's mood. But not mine.

"I was thinking, there's another place only half a mile from here." Jamila could barely contain her excitement.

"Um, okay."

Jamila scrutinized me. "You're bored, aren't you?"

"Well ..."

She smiled and shook her head. "Guess you and I won't be watching *Antiques Roadshow* together anytime soon."

"I'd take that bet."

φφφ

We stopped for coffee then drove to the condo and parked in the lot. A group of twenty-somethings stood around a candy-apple red Corvette. They turned to look at us as we got out of the car. I recognized a couple of them. Renters in the condo beneath ours. They'd kept the stereo blasting until well after midnight the night before. I'd gone down and threatened to sic the cops on them. They had slammed the door in my face. I'd stomped back upstairs and made the call. I suspected I wasn't high on their list of favorite people.

"Hey!" one of the men called out. "You ain't supposed to park here 'less you live here."

"We're renters. We have permission," I shot back, not stopping to engage him further. *How is this your damn business, anyway? Who are you, the parking lot police?*

"Well, that's a fine thing," the young man shouted. "Didn't know niggers could rent here."

I ignored him, but I could feel my face grow hot with anger. The group snickered amongst themselves. A real rocket scientist, I mused. Probably a Harvard grad.

"Hey!" he said again. "I'm talking to you."

The guy ran around and barred our entry to the exterior staircase leading to our unit. Jamila and I froze. I gazed at the gangly, sandy-blond kid. A real shit-kicker, based on looks alone. Grin a bit too goofy, beady eyes a bit too close set. His parents were probably first cousins.

"I said, I didn't know *niggers* could rent here." He challenged Jamila with a withering look. Then it was my turn.

I stared right back. I was ready to kick his nuts up to his neck. But all his friends were there. Things could get ugly. So I did nothing.

Jamila was a vision of total calm. She didn't even flinch when he used the N-word.

I whipped out my cell phone. "Step aside or I call the cops."

"And have me arrested? For what, you dumb white bitch?" The blond began laughing. All his friends joined in.

He had a point. He hadn't done much of anything. Yet.

"Excuse me," Jamila said, trying to get past him.

"Whoa, whoa! Don't be pushing me around, girl. That's battery, you know."

The others had drifted over. Guess they didn't want to miss the big show.

I eyed them surreptitiously. Two guys and two girls. All white. All corn-fed inbreds.

The young man peered at me. "You're the one called the cops on us, ain't ya?"

"Yes, I'm the one," I said. "So why don't you leave my friend out of it? And try not playing your music so loud you wake up people in Philadelphia."

"I didn't break no rules. I can play music as loud as I want."

"Local ordinances say otherwise." Ocean City had noise ordinances because of the overabundance of "June bugs" (the local term for rowdy high school kids doing their "school's out" ritual) and bikers on Harleys with straight pipes.

"Well, being that my daddy owns the building, I think I ought to know what I can and can't do."

Oh, Christ. I'd about had it with the little shit. Jamila continued to look stoic, standing proudly erect.

"Your daddy may own the place, but you can't just ignore the law." *Asshole.*

Once again, Jamila tried to maneuver around the tall blond. He grabbed at the container Jamila held. A brief tussle ensued before he wrested it from her hand.

"What's this?" He tore the box open and tossed it aside. The wrapping paper sailed off on the breeze. "Well, ain't that cute?" He surveyed the antique music box like he'd unearthed it from an archeological dig.

"Hey, check this out, guys." He waved the music box around.

The group drew closer. Their eyes were vacant. They simply followed the leader.

Jeez! What is this? Day of the Dead? The Ocean City Zombie Brigade?

"So, tell me," the young man said. "How does a nigger afford a fancy car and a fancy box like this?"

Jamila stayed silent for a long moment. "Give that back," she finally said, in a firm voice.

"How do I know it's yours? You probably stole it."

The group snickered again. They sounded like a pit of rattlesnakes.

I was losing it, so I tried to snatch the box. The kid threw it to someone in the group. They tossed it back and forth like a hot potato.

Jamila's look never wavered, but I could sense desperation, worry, and anger. The two male friends circled around me and Jamila as they played catch with their leader.

I tried to make another grab for the box as it sailed past. It bounced off my fingers and smashed on the pavement. The delicate inlay shattered. The box lay scratched and splintered. And no amount of Krazy Glue could repair it.

A string of curse words passed through my mind. Jamila retained her impassive expression, but I knew she probably wanted to cry. I wanted to impale myself on the nearest stake.

"Don't go blaming me for that," the young man taunted. "I'da caught it, if you hadn't gotten in the way."

"And this whole thing wouldn't be happening if you hadn't grabbed it and started throwing it around, you ass wipe." I'd reached my limit.

"Aren't you the tough girl?" The young man lorded it over me.

"Why don't you leave them be, Billy Ray?" The voice was female, faltering and soft. The face was pretty, the hair light brown and shoulder length, the eyes hazel and sincere.

"Don't be telling me what to do, Danni!" The kid snapped. "You ain't my girl no more. You can't be bossing me around."

"Well, isn't she the lucky one?" I muttered into Jamila's ear. She gave the ghost of a smile.

"What did you say?" Billy Ray turned his rabid, beady gaze my way.

"Just sharing my thoughts about you. Nothing important."

Billy Ray didn't catch the obvious slam. Nor did he budge.

"She's right, Billy Ray." One of the other guys spoke up. "Let's blow this pop stand."

"Hmmph." Billy Ray looked disgusted. "Fine thing, when a nigger and her little white girlfriend can make me leave my daddy's property."

He continued to stand in our way.

"C'mon, Billy Ray!" The other girl whined. "I'm bored."

The whiner was a pretty redhead with fair skin, green eyes, and big tits, which she showcased to great advantage in a tight tank top.

"Well ..." he said.

"I want to leave now!" the redhead demanded.

"Hey, Billy Ray," one of the guys said. "That *is* your girl talking. Wanna get any tonight or not?"

The boys chuckled. I glanced between Billy Ray and Big Red. He looked torn by indecision. She stared him down and crossed her arms beneath her breasts, pushing them up to her chin.

I felt sick, shuddering to think how these pathetic losers must live. Big Red seemed to be enjoying her hold over Billy Ray. *Jesus, girl! Get a life.*

Billy Ray nodded decisively, as if he was in charge. "Yeah, let's get the hell out of here. This is getting dull."

As he stalked off, Big Red glided toward him and grabbed his arm, like a drowning woman lunging at a flotation device.

"We're having another party tonight," he shot over his shoulder at us. "We'll try to keep it down so you old folks can sleep."

The others guffawed as they followed him—all except Danni. The quiet girl held back long enough to say, "It's not even his daddy. It's his stepdaddy." She ran to join the others piling into the red Corvette.

CHAPTER THREE

Jamila said nothing as we climbed the stairs and let ourselves in. I cleared my throat. "I guess the Welcome Wagon has changed its approach."

Jamila walked to the sliding glass door leading to the balcony and simply stared. Apparently, my attempt at humor wasn't cutting it.

I tried to think of something—anything—else to say. I failed.

Sighing, I parked myself on the couch and hit the TV remote. I had to create some noise or the silence would deafen me.

Jamila kept her watch at the window, surveying the bay's waters as if expecting a Navy Seal attack.

I flipped through channels, interested in nothing.

"You know, I used to live in Salisbury."

Jamila's words jolted me. I muted the sound and dropped the remote in my lap.

"I didn't know you were from the Eastern Shore."

"Oh, yeah." She sighed. "My family hasn't been back since we moved to D.C. It's been years. They always preferred to vacation on Martha's Vineyard."

"I've never been there," I said.

"It's beautiful. So's Nantucket." She kept staring out the window.

"A lot of … well-to-do people go there," I said. Filthy rich people, I thought. The kind who would look at me with disdain or, even worse, pity as a child living in the worst part of Brooklyn.

"My family was well-to-do." She spit the words at the window. "*Is*, I should say. Money hasn't been a problem for a long time. My parents have made sure of that. They were raised to become better than their own parents."

I nodded, even though she wasn't looking.

"All their money, their influence, their good friends," Jamila continued. "But they can't change one thing. They'll never be white. And neither will I."

I grimaced. "You don't want to be white. It's boring."

A grin twisted the corners of Jamila's lips. But when she turned to me, the grin had gone lopsided. "I could stand for that kind of boredom right about now."

"I know. Believe me, I do." I looked her in the eye. "I've told you about how I used to be the only white kid in Bed-Stuy, right? Would it shock you to know that I used to wish I was black?"

Jamila shook her head. "You don't want to be black. It's anything but boring."

φφφ

The next day, we planned to spend time hanging around Assateague. Jamila hoped to catch a glimpse of wild ponies or egrets or blue herons. It all sounded very charming, as long as we brought along enough mosquito repellent and sunscreen. I wish I could call myself a nature lover, but I tend to go more for pictures of the great outdoors than its actuality.

After smearing my exposed skin with SPF-80, I pulled on a floppy hat to keep the sun's rays from barbecuing my face.

"Do I need to bring a machete?" I asked.

"You are a laugh riot," Jamila said, inserting a last barrette. "Don't worry. We'll stick to the trails." She had her hair pinned up and was decked out in jeans, a short-sleeved shirt and sturdy hiking boots appropriate for a Borneo jungle trek.

We gathered our goods—water canisters, a camera, binoculars, granola bars, fruit rollups, and a couple of packages of M&Ms (my contribution)—and made our way down to the parking lot. Which looked to be asshole free.

As we crossed the lot, the candy-apple red Corvette pulled into the driveway. Billy Ray and his cohorts making a return appearance.

"Oh, fuck!" I muttered, between gritted teeth.

"Ignore them," Jamila said, as we proceeded to the car.

Instead of pulling all the way into the lot, the Corvette stopped in the entrance.

Billy Ray leaned out the window. "Hey, you guys going somewhere?"

Well, duh! "We can't go much of anywhere if you don't move your car."

"You really shouldn't have called the cops on us," Billy Ray goaded.

And you should shut your fucking mouth and leave us alone. God, I was dying to say it.

Billy Ray opened the door, unfolded himself from the car and began walking toward us.

"I realize niggers can be slow, but you gals really need to understand your place here." He swaggered as he spoke.

"That's it!" I pulled out my cell phone and hit 911.

"Whatta you think you're doing?" Billy Ray asked.

"Calling the cops, shithead. You're blocking a public thoroughfare. I'm sure there's a ticket in it for you somewhere."

Billy Ray ignored me and swaggered right up to Jamila, who looked frozen in place. I noticed his gang huddled in the car, watching.

"Well, don't you look nice?" he said, grinning in her face.

Jamila merely stared back, eyes blank.

I knew what she was up to. Jamila refused to sink to the level of other people's ignorance. She was playing Jackie Robinson to Billy Ray's Ty Cobb. The rest of us were like spectators to a Mexican standoff.

"Still, I liked your hair better when it was down." Billy's arm shot out like a sideways jack-in-the-box. He snatched at her hair. The other arm followed and repeated the exercise, over and over. Jamila raised her hands to fight him off, but he kept evading them. He must have pulled a couple of combs and a barrette from her hair before she finally hauled off and slapped him.

"Nine-one-one. Please state the nature of your emergency."

The phone. "I'd like to report an assault and battery," I said. "I'd also like to bring false arrest charges—"

"Yes, ma'am." She cut me off. "I'll need your address."

"Fifty-five three seventeen Bayview Avenue. And please hurry."

CHAPTER FOUR

By the time the cruiser arrived, Billy Ray and his zombie brigade were gone. The cop who responded looked to be about sixteen. He and Billy Ray could have attended high school together. Maybe sat in the same homeroom. Compared notes on the same girls.

The kid—the cop, that is—walked up to us, a quizzical look in his baby blues.

"Did one of you call about a disturbance?"

I raised a hand. "I did. The disturbers have hit the frickin' bricks."

Jamila counted her barrettes and combs, shaking her head. "One's missing." She squatted to peer beneath the cars again.

The cop's brow furrowed. He scratched it with his pen. "I can file a report, if you'd like." His tone suggested, "Why bother?"

"I think we should," I told Jamila.

"Why?" She squat-stepped sideways, ducking her head and doing another visual sweep. Finally, she straightened and added, sounding annoyed, "What good will it do? We don't even know his full name?"

"Ah, but I got his tag number."

Jamila did a double-take and smiled. "Quick thinking, Sam. Way to go."

I hoped that my quick thinking would help make up for the inadvertent damage to her music box. I didn't realize it would just lead to more trouble.

Who knew that Billy Ray, aka William Raymond Wesley, would end up knifed in the gut while passed out on the downstairs porch that night? Or that someone would plant Jamila's comb near his body?

Filing the report provided more evidence of animosity between Jamila and the deceased. Surely, not enough for her to commit murder, I argued to the cops. My words fell on deaf ears. Before I knew it, they'd arranged a lineup. A witness fingered Jamila as the one he'd seen at the scene of the crime hours earlier. As they led my friend away to be fingerprinted, I realized we needed local counsel. We were both outsiders and city slickers. Neither of us knew the local ropes or had the proper connections to handle this.

φφφ

A couple of hours after they'd taken her, I was allowed to see Jamila. In the visiting room, it felt more than a bit peculiar to see her in an orange jumpsuit seated on the wrong side of the table.

"I've called Rudy and my parents." Jamila sounded tired.

"I can only imagine how they must feel."

Jamila blew out a breath. Her shoulders sagged, her body deflated. "Not good. Rudy hasn't told the kids."

"Hopefully, he won't have to. You realize, of course, we've got to hire a local attorney."

Jamila raised her index finger. "I used one of my calls to reach my father. He recommended someone he worked with here years ago."

Sounded hopeful. Jamila's father was an attorney at one of D.C.'s biggest firms. "Who?"

"His name is Edward G. Mulrooney."

"If he's as impressive as his name, he should be good."

φφφ

I called Mulrooney. Jamila's father had already hired him to cover her bail hearing later that morning. With that out of the way, I arranged in the wee hours to move into temporary quarters since our condo was still off-limits and crawling with crime techs. I scrounged up a motel on Coastal Highway near the Delaware line. It was late (or early) and vacancies were few and far between, so I took the room without close inspection. I stumbled through the door, threw myself on one of two double beds, and drifted off for a few hours. I woke up in a musty, oversized closet passing itself off as a room.

I heaved myself off the bed with a grunt and trudged to the window. A peek through the curtains revealed a canal lined with a chain link fence and scrubby grass. The stagnant waters reflected the murky dark sky.

"Charming." My voice sounded like the bottom of a shoe scraping against a curb.

Splashing water on my face, I rinsed out my mouth and tried to tidy up before heading downtown to attend the bail hearing.

φφφ

Things went about as well as could be expected. Bail was set at $5 million—a heart-stopping figure, but not for Jamila's parents. They'd probably manage to cover the bond.

Mulrooney arranged to see Jamila after the hearing. When she insisted I sit in on the meeting, Mulrooney wasn't thrilled. However, she persuaded him to take me on as pro bono co-counsel to cover confidentiality concerns. I also made it clear I had no desire to steal Mulrooney's thunder.

For my own part, I was glad to let him take the lead and play second fiddle.

We met in a visiting room painted in soothing shades of doody-diaper green and furnished with the latest in institutional gray metal table and chairs.

Mulrooney was a country lawyer straight from Central Casting. White hair, wire-rimmed glasses, seersucker suit, pleasant demeanor with a glint in his eyes that suggested intelligence buried beneath the country corn.

"Your father," Mulrooney said to Jamila. "That man could pick crabs like no one else."

"God, yes. He loves crabs," Jamila said. "Oysters and rockfish, too."

"And ribs?" Mulrooney tilted his head back, letting his jaw drop. A raucous laugh echoed through the visiting room. "That man could suck every last piece of meat off a rib. Or a chicken wing, for that matter."

Jamila smiled politely. I checked my watch. It had been nearly ten minutes of chitchat. How long were we going to discuss Jamila's dad and his dietary habits? Would we move onto his bathroom habits next?

"Now." The sound of the word ricocheted around the room like a rifle shot. Mulrooney's gaze bored into Jamila over his wire-rims. "Let's talk about your case."

"So soon?" I muttered.

I didn't think I'd been audible, but Jamila threw me a look. Mulrooney either didn't hear or chose to ignore me.

"The police have shared some of the evidence they've turned up with me. Unfortunately, there is an eyewitness—"

Jamila shook her head. "Does this witness claim he saw me kill the victim?"

Mulrooney held up a hand. "Let's take this one step at a time, shall we?"

He leaned back in his chair and steepled his fingers. I took a deep breath and blew it out slowly, as he spoke. "The body was discovered at approximately 11:30 P.M. on the front porch of the condo beneath yours. According to his friends, they'd been having a party. Wesley had so much to drink that when the others decided to get something to eat, he could barely walk. Apparently, they left him passed out on the porch in a lounge chair.

"Now." He nearly shouted the word again and paused before continuing. "According to these friends, they left around 10:30 and didn't return for about an hour. That's when they found him. He was still in the lounge chair, bleeding from his gut. A gruesome death." He shook his head. "A horrible crime."

I yawned deliberately. "Boo hoo."

Mulrooney swiveled his laser gaze toward me. "You should have more respect for the dead, Ms. McRae."

"And the dead should have had more respect for my friend. Could we possibly—" I made circles with my finger in a speed-it-up gesture.

Mulrooney's look never wavered. "Respect. It's an important thing to remember here. People respect Wesley's family. That *will* be a factor."

Rather than ask, I gave an inward sigh and awaited his explanation.

He turned back to Jamila. "As I was saying, the friends called the police upon finding the deceased. After the cops arrived, a passerby on a bicycle approached them. He claimed he'd seen someone coming down the stairs and slipping into the shadows on the front porch. This witness also thought it appeared to be a tall, slender woman. Dark complexion. That was the sum and substance of the description. When he picked you out of the lineup, that's when they decided to go for the arrest."

"This is all very fascinating," I interrupted. "But what about the forensics? What about all the blood? If Jamila had done this, wouldn't there be evidence of blood in the condo? Or on her clothes?"

"Ah." Mulrooney held up a didactic finger. "The police found bloody clothing."

"They did?" This was news.

"After the lineup, they asked Jamila to identify some clothing they'd found near the crime scene."

Jamila shook her head. "I told them, they could be anyone's and wouldn't say more without legal counsel."

"A wise move," Mulrooney observed, nodding her way. To me, he said, "They found a pair of women's jeans, a T-shirt and tennis shoes, along with the knife in the dumpster next door. There was blood all over them."

CHAPTER FIVE

"Big deal," I said. "So they found some bloody clothing and a knife next door from where he died. How does this prove anything against Jamila?"

Mulrooney turned toward me and raised his finger—his index finger, for the record—again. "Patience."

I bit my tongue and exercised all the patience I could muster.

"Now," Mulrooney stated with irritating repetition. "Naturally, they're testing to make sure the blood matches that of the victim. Those results may take a couple of days. Assuming the blood matches, they may want hair samples for DNA testing. That kind of testing doesn't come cheap. However, in this case, they may find the cost justified. It'll depend on how strong the other evidence is. For instance, when the police searched the condo you're renting, they noticed a knife missing from the butcher block." His look bored into Jamila. "Did you realize that?"

Jamila shook her head. "I never noticed. Sam?"

I spread my hands, feeling helpless. "Are you kidding? I barely noticed the kitchen." As Jamila knew, I'm hardly the domestic sort. My idea of cooking is heating frozen entrees or leftover Chinese.

"Unfortunately, the knife appears to be part of the set in your kitchen."

For a moment, neither of us spoke.

I cleared my throat. "Do you know how many similar sets of cutlery could be out there? How do they know it's from our set?"

"The fact that the knife is missing doesn't help."

"Oh, come on." I lost it at this point. "The killer could have broken in and stolen it. If it was one of the victim's friends, they saw what happened between Jamila and that racist son of a bitch. In fact, the victim's stepfather owns the place. The killer could have filched a key from him."

I paused to gather my thoughts. My words were making me sound like a conspiracy theorist and I wasn't sure if Mulrooney was buying.

"Apart from speculating about the knife and clothes, is there anything linking the murder directly to Jamila?" I asked. "Any forensic evidence?"

"Here's where it gets a little interesting."

As if it weren't already.

"The police not only found her comb near the body, but they found traces of blood on the front porch of your condo. Again, they're awaiting the test results, but if it's the victim's blood …"

Jamila and I both fell quiet.

"Wait a second," I said. "If Jamila threw out the bloody clothing, how could she leave traces of blood on the porch? Someone is obviously setting her up."

Mulrooney sighed. "I, for one, am willing to believe you. However, others will be more difficult to convince. They will likely argue that blood got on her hands as she was removing her clothes."

"Sure, they will probably argue that, but she could be looking at first-degree murder. Now what would be her motive? And don't say racism. Jamila wouldn't go to such lengths to kill a man simply because he was a racist, would she?"

Mulrooney fixed me with a thoughtful look. He leaned toward Jamila. "Can you think of a motive?"

Jamila started to speak, then stopped. She avoided eye contact.

"Yes." Mulrooney agreed, but I had no idea what he was agreeing to.

"What is it?" I asked.

Mulrooney looked at our client—my friend. Jamila didn't answer.

φφφ

Before we finished, Mulrooney said he'd arrange to hire a local investigator. He said he knew just the man: Ellis Conroy. If anyone could find evidence to poke holes in the prosecution's case, it would be Conroy. Before we left, I made sure to get Conroy's number. I couldn't help but feel panicked. I had to do something. I couldn't simply sit back and wait for Conroy to work his magic. On top of that, Jamila had never answered my question. *What could she be withholding?*

"Let's keep in touch." Mulrooney tossed the suggestion out as he strolled to his car, a blue Caddy with all the trimmings. He threw his briefcase onto the passenger seat and walked around to the driver's side. "I'm heading to a meeting, but I'll get on the phone with her father right now and arrange for her bail. I'm sure he can cover it."

"I'll call Conroy," I said. "Perhaps I can help." *Meanwhile, could you please tell me what the hell just happened?*

"Fine," Mulrooney stated as he pulled a cell phone from its holster and slid into the car. "Not to discourage you, but Conroy is a fine investigator. I'm sure he's capable of handling this on his own."

I wracked my brain for a response. It felt like fishing in barren waters.

"I … just hate sitting back and doing nothing," I said, for lack of a better thought.

"Hmm." Mulrooney hummed like a pipe organ. "I understand. Just be sure to coordinate whatever you do with Ellis."

"Um, it might help if I knew what motivation you were talking about in there. Or, actually, *not* talking about."

Mulrooney got that thoughtful look again. "I'd … like the client to make the call on revealing that."

Oh, great. "Are you sure that won't make my job harder?"

"It won't," he assured me. "In a sense, it should make it easier." With that, he shut the door.

I nodded and turned toward Jamila's car, thinking *I hope to hell you're right.*

φφφ

I drove toward Ocean City with thoughts of the Maryland State Bar Association's convention worming their way into my consciousness. I assumed Jamila's parents wouldn't have a problem with the bail bond. Even so, the bond on $5 million bail wasn't chump change. On top of that, she was supposed to give a presentation on ethics in four days.

How ironic was that? How would it look if news of her arrest came out? For that matter, had it already?

I pulled into the lot of a convenience store and bought a local paper. As I walked, I flipped through the pages, nearly tripping over a toddler. His mother glared at me.

"I … I'm sorry," I sputtered.

She shook her head. "People should pay more attention. They read when they drive, they talk on phones and text. What could be so all-fired important in that paper?"

"My best friend's been accused of murder. Excuse me, ma'am."

I beat a hasty retreat, feeling her stare boring into my back.

φφφ

Once I'd gotten to the car, I riffled through the paper. Nothing in the first few pages. Good. I flipped to an inside section and my heart sank. A headline screamed across the top of the page: "Visiting Attorney Arrested for Murder of Local Magnate's Stepson."

While the lead described her only as "an attorney in town for the annual Maryland State Bar Association convention," her name and age were revealed farther down. Along with the fact that she'd filed a report with the police about the decedent, who as it turned out was the stepson of Marshall Bower, a local entrepreneur with a finger in every pie in town.

CHAPTER SIX

Okay, I thought. It's Tuesday. The convention doesn't officially start until tomorrow. Even then, most people don't show up on the very first day. A lot of people will miss this.

Then, I realized the local broadcast media would be on this like hounds on a fox. Like vultures on road kill, to be more precise.

"Shit!" I threw the paper aside. "Why did you have to be some rich guy's stepson?" Frustration and rage rose in my throat. I smacked the heel of my hand on the wheel several times. People walking past my car slowed and stared at me.

I took a couple of deep breaths. My hand shook slightly as I turned the ignition, but I started the car. I even managed to pull a shit-eating grin and give the gawkers a brief salute before I left.

φφφ

En route to our lovely new digs, I hit a drugstore to pick up a few essentials and then swung past the convention center to scope out whether the conference organizers had cottoned to the news of Jamila's arrest. As I suspected, few of my peers were in evidence. While some of them may have chosen to use the convention as an excuse to take a week's vacation, I was sure most were only taking a few days off from busy schedules to be here. That's the practice of law for you: just one long nonstop party.

I ventured into the cavernous building, wandering past a long line of display tables, still empty but no doubt soon to be filled with process servers, title examiners, litigation support services, and other hungry vendors. As I glanced around, a familiar voice came from behind me. One I didn't particularly want to hear.

"Sam? Sam McRae, is that you?"

I turned to face the source. "Hello, Jinx."

Jingle Henderson had to be one of the most irritating lawyers I'd ever known. Her nickname couldn't have been more appropriate. There was no rule Jinx wouldn't try to bend—nearly to the breaking point. I'd dealt with her bullshit on more than one occasion. I didn't want to deal with it now.

However, instead of the cool reception she usually gave me, Jinx beamed a broad smile in my direction. She rushed me and threw her arms around me like a linebacker.

"It's so good to see you, Sam," she said.

"Uh huh." That's all I could force myself to say, as my mind screamed, *what the fuck?*

Jinx loosened her grip and stepped back, still grinning. "We need to talk."

Must we? "About what?"

Jinx's expression turned more solemn. "Would you like to get coffee?"

Though I'm second to none in my love of coffee, the thought of having it with Jinx wasn't enticing. I let her question hang for a moment before answering. Should I refuse? I'll admit, I was curious.

"Okay. Where do you want to go?"

"There's a place about a mile from here on the boardwalk. Java on the Beach. Do you know it? I could drive us."

Again, I pondered an appropriate reply. I suspected it wasn't, "Gee, Jinx, that's nice, but I'd rather walk there barefoot over broken glass than be stuck in the same car with you."

Finally, I said, "I know the place. Would it be okay if we met there in an hour or so? I'm looking for someone." Anyone else.

Jinx nodded so fast it made me dizzy.

"Awesome! Let's exchange numbers." Reluctantly, I gave her mine and programmed hers into my phone. She glanced at her watch. "See you in about an hour then?"

I nodded as she walked away. *Now what's going on?*

CHAPTER SEVEN

I continued my search for the program coordinator. Jamila was scheduled to make her presentation Saturday afternoon. Mulrooney should be able to arrange her release well before then. Even so, I wondered if anyone associated with the conference had read the local papers. Or how they would react to news reports that night.

For a frozen moment, I worried about word getting out through the new social media. Facebook, and now something called Twitter. But who used that stuff? Kids. Ha!

Traditional media and the rumor mill were my bigger concerns. How would it look for Jamila to give a lecture on ethics after being arrested as a murder suspect? Would the program planner want to cancel her session?

In a far corner, I spied Betsy Larkin, the program coordinator, deep in consultation with a red-faced man in a tight-fitting suit. He didn't look happy. I approached with caution, not wanting to interrupt.

"I asked for bottled water," Betsy said. "You know, the cute little bottles? Everyone loves them."

As Betsy made her pitch for cute little bottles of water, I wondered if this was the right time to bring up another possible glitch in the program.

"Also," Betsy said, "I was hoping for a wider variety of fruit juices with the morning pastries and coffee."

While Betsy rambled through her culinary demands, I pondered the notion that it might be unwise to broach the subject of Jamila's problems. After all, I had four days. She might be eliminated as a suspect in that time.

"Have you got that?" Betsy concluded to the flustered-looking man. As he bustled off, Betsy aimed her formidable figure my way.

Standing roughly six feet in low heels with a gray helmet of hair, Betsy gave the distinct aura of one not to be trifled with. She looked down at me, a skulking 5-foot, 8-inch midget, and said, "What can I do for you?"

Don't hit me. I'm ashamed to admit they were the first words that came to mind. "I … uh, I just wanted to say you've put together a great program. I can't wait for the sessions to start."

Betsy looked thunderstruck. "Why … why thank you. That's very nice. What did you say your name was?"

"I didn't, but it's Sam McRae."

"Well, Sam, it's really good to meet you." Betsy pumped my hand and nearly wrenched my arm from its socket.

I opted for the time being to keep mum about Jamila.

φφφ

As I left the convention center, I ran into Kaitlyn Farrell from the State's Attorney's Office.

"What are you doing here so early?" I asked.

"I'm a presenter, remember?" I recalled then that Kait was giving a tutorial on recent criminal law developments. "I had the leave and I needed a break from the grind, so I'm here early to get a little R&R before my big presentation." She said the last two words, using finger quotes. "I figured I'd stop by and check out what's going on." She peered into the nearly empty building, shook her head and turned toward me. "Not much, from the looks of it."

"The place will be more lively later this week," I assured her. "Can't wait to hear you." I tried to recollect when she was scheduled.

"I guess Ray will be basking in it this weekend," Kait said, rolling her eyes. Ray Mardovich was a state's attorney with whom I'd had an adulterous fling almost a year ago. Things had ended on a sour note—especially when I discovered he'd been seeing yet another woman. Now, the once-divorced, soon-to-be-twice-married Ray was to be installed on Saturday as the new bar association president. This amazed me on more levels than I cared to ponder.

It took all my restraint not to spout expletives. "I'm sure he'll do a great job."

"He is the kind of guy who can get things done."

"Yes," I said. "He's a real politician. Always trying to please everyone."

For good or ill, the irony of that statement was lost.

φφφ

As I slid behind the wheel of my car, my cell phone jangled. To my surprise, it was Jinx.

"Sam, I wonder if we could reschedule our meeting. Would tomorrow afternoon be okay? Say, around 1:30?"

"Sure. That's fine."

"Oh, good. I can't wait."

As we hung up, I breathed a sigh. *Well, I can.*

I then punched in the number for our crack investigator, Conroy. Four rings later, he picked up.

"Hi. This is Sam McRae."

"Mulrooney told me you'd be calling." The voice was low and brusque and the line came out so fast, it sounded practiced.

"Would you have a moment to meet now?"

"Sure. C'mon by, if you like."

If I like? Yes, I think I would. I got directions to his place before ending the call.

From the convention center, I took a left and headed north on Coastal Highway, the town's Main Street, past iterations of strip shopping centers and miniature golf courses adorned with faux palm trees and waterfalls. Toward the north end of town, tall condo buildings stood sentry-like, their facades glowing in the setting sun.

Conroy worked from his home office on the bay side: 2555 Pine Shore Lane. I made a left at Pine Shore and looked for 2555. It was a small cottage. White with light blue trim. A dark blue Toyota parked out front. The street dead-ended a few hundred feet from the house. Nice and quiet, with no through traffic. The kind of house a retiree might prefer. I wondered how old Conroy might be.

I went up the walk and knocked on a front door flanked by rose bushes, their salmon pink and orange flowers perfuming the air. The walk bisected the yard into two small scrubby green squares. Apart from the low white noise of distant traffic, the occasional shrieks of gulls were the only sound. I stood and watched a pelican dive for the bay. As it swooped in, I heard a voice rumble behind me.

"Can I help you?"

I snapped around. A man about my height stood in the doorway. Late fifties, thinning hair. Face brown and wrinkled with the squint of a fisherman, a skeptic, or both. He grinned at my discomfiture.

"Or did you just come to admire the scenery?" he asked.

φφφ

After we'd exchanged introductions, Conroy led me to his office in a converted garage. The desk was weighed down by piles of paper. He picked a stack of folders off a chair and nodded toward it. I sat. I'm not the most organized person, but Conroy's office made me look fastidious.

"Coffee? Tea? Water?" he asked.

"Coffee would be nice."

"Sugar? Milk?"

"Just black."

"Good. Cause that's all I've got. I don't even have fucking milk." He laughed. "Pardon my French."

"Don't worry about it."

"Good. I won't fucking worry about it then." He guffawed. I smiled in return. He poured a Styrofoam cup of brew from a carafe on a side table.

He landed in his chair and propped his feet on the desk. "So, how can I help you?"

"I was hoping I could help you."

He frowned and squinted harder. "Exactly how?"

"I think my friend's been framed for murder. I want to help find out who really did this."

His face scrunched so hard, it seemed near to imploding. "You're a lawyer, aren't you?"

"Uh, yeah."

"You know you don't have to prove her innocence then."

"But if we can find evidence that someone else did this and eliminate Jamila as a suspect, the matter could get dismissed. She could expunge the arrest from her record—like it never happened."

He sighed and swung his feet off the desk. Leaning toward me, he said, "Well, sure. But what's this 'we' stuff? I work alone, understand?"

"I'm just trying to help."

He shook his head. "Look here, girlie. I've been doing this for almost thirty years. I've lived here all my life. If I can't get the job done, I doubt anyone can."

Um, excuse me?

"Well, first of all, my name is Sam—"

"Now, you're not going to get your undies in a twist over a little expression, are you?"

"And second," I continued. "I can't sit back and simply do nothing."

"Well, fine. Knock yourself out. But, I don't want or need your help. And, believe me, you won't get far around here on your own."

There was a distinct challenge in his words that put me on edge.

"This is a very close-knit community," he droned. "I know the ins and outs. And I have the contacts. With all due respect, you don't."

"Fair enough," I said, holding back a plethora of acidic responses. "But if there's anything I *can* do—"

He coughed up a laugh. "Look, I know you wanna help your friend, okay? But I'm the professional. I'll get right on this and be reporting to Mulrooney on a regular basis. Okay?"

"And I'm telling you as his co-counsel that I intend to be involved in some way." *You patronizing bastard.*

"You want to help?" He coughed out another laugh, then jabbed a finger at me. "The best way to help me is to just stay out of my fucking way. You got that, girlie?" He came down heavy on the last word.

I rose. "Thanks for the fucking coffee." I turned and left.

φφφ

As I started my car, my phone rang. It was Mulrooney. Jamila's parents had come through on the bail bond. I aimed my car toward Coastal Highway and headed directly for the jail.

As I left Conroy's, I was steaming. *That sexist son of a bitch!* Good thing I had several blocks to bring my full-boil anger down to a low simmer before reaching my destination. When I got there, Mulrooney was awaiting Jamila's release. This was the good news. Unfortunately, the bad news had hit the local radio stations. No doubt Jamila's arrest would be on everyone's lips tomorrow. Thank God most of the convention's attendees probably wouldn't roll in until the day after or Friday. Would this still be news by then?

Jamila emerged and collected her things, looking dazed. Mulrooney placed a hand on her shoulder.

"Go home. Get some rest," he said. "Let's meet at my office tomorrow. Say around nine?"

We both nodded.

I led Jamila out to the car, got behind the wheel and headed back to the motel. I made sure to keep the radio off.

She sat silent, arms crossed, staring straight ahead.

"Are you all right?" My words sounded feeble and idiotic.

Jamila just nodded. I didn't press.

As we drove, the only sounds were roller coasters clattering, motorcycles roaring, kids laughing. The farther north we went, the more traffic noises took over. Buses wheezing, horns honking.

Once we'd arrived at the motel, its seediness didn't seem to register on Jamila's radar. Eyes glazed, moving like a robot, she exited the car and trailed me to the room. I opened the door, and she took zombielike steps inside. She dropped her shoulder bag on the floor without looking, walked to the closest bed and abruptly sat on it.

Planting her elbows on her thighs, she buried her face in her hands.

"I don't believe this," she said.

When she lifted her face, I saw it was streaked with tears. I rushed to sit beside her and hugged her.

"Don't worry," I said. "You're innocent, goddamn it. We're going to get you out of this. Free and clear."

I was still dying to ask about the unspoken exchange between her and Mulrooney, but this hardly seemed like the right time. So I ignored the doubt nibbling at my gut.

CHAPTER EIGHT

The sun shone in a China blue sky as Jamila and I drove to Salisbury the next morning. A salty breeze blew through the car. Seagulls wheeled and squawked in airborne choreography as we left the ocean, crossed the Route 50 Bridge and motored inland.

Mulrooney's office was near the courthouse, but our first stop was a coffee shop down the street. Mulrooney was there, chatting up the cashier.

"Mornin', ladies," he said, with a nod and a smile.

"Hey," I said.

As I scanned the pastry selections, Mulrooney nudged me and said, "I'm a cheese Danish man, myself."

I smiled, nodded. Why not? I ordered one with a large cup of dark roast coffee to go.

After we paid, Mulrooney led us on foot to his office. People smiled and waved at him, and he beamed and returned the greeting. *Where am I, Mayberry?*

Mulrooney's office was in an old brick building where George Washington probably slept. As we entered, he told his secretary, "Becky, please hold all my calls," before we proceeded past her desk and into his inner sanctum. He switched on a small oscillating fan atop a file cabinet, walked behind his desk, and dropped into his chair. Jamila and I each settled into a seat facing him.

"Here's the situation," Mulrooney intoned, perching his elbows on the armrests and steepling his fingers. "Right now, a preliminary hearing is scheduled in two weeks. As you know," he said, nodding toward me, "the matter could still get dismissed. However, if the blood on the clothing matches the victim's, they will probably look for confirmation in DNA tests on it. If there's a match, we've got a problem."

"If there's a match, the clothing must have been stolen," I said. "Along with the knife."

Good grief! I sounded like a candidate for a tin foil hat.

I wanted to say Jamila had an alibi. She was with me. But we were in separate rooms. I couldn't account for her whereabouts. Anyhow, who would believe me?

I wracked my brain, but other than standard arguments for excluding evidence, I wasn't sure exactly what to suggest.

"I met with Ellis Conroy," I said. "I was hoping we could work together to find a way to clear Jamila. But he doesn't seem terribly open."

"Why am I not surprised?" Mulrooney looked grim. "The man is a curmudgeon."

"That's one way of putting it," I said.

Mulrooney smiled. "Yes. Well."

He scribbled a note on his pad.

"Now," he said. He really liked that word. "I don't want to unduly scare you, but we need to be prepared for the worst."

"What do you mean?" Jamila asked.

"Here's the problem in a nutshell. We're dealing with a high-profile murder involving a well-established family. There is some political pressure to bear on the State's Attorney's Office to prosecute this case with all due speed."

"I take it the lack of a speedy trial won't be a problem," Jamila said.

"If anything, quite the opposite."

"But all they have is a bloody knife and clothing, which may have been stolen from us, a comb that Jamila lost, blood on the porch that someone went out of their way to plant and a possibly unreliable eyewitness." I took a breath. Okay, that was quite a bit. "They also have no motive," I added, waiting for the elderly attorney to supply one.

Mulrooney sighed. "There's another thing."

No. Not another thing.

"My sources tell me hairs were found on the clothing. Coarse, dark hairs." He looked at Jamila and sighed. "You can bet they'll do DNA testing on those."

I shook my head, as if it could wipe everything away. "They could've gotten those off her comb." Seemed like a reasonable explanation. To me, anyhow. Would it just sound like an excuse to someone else?

Mulrooney gazed at me with a thoughtful expression. "There's more to this than simply the evidence. We're dealing with a highly influential Eastern Shore family."

My jaw dropped. "What's that have to do with anything?" Like I didn't know.

Mulrooney grunted. "Marshall Bower and his son, Junior, carry a lot of political clout. Now, assuming the DNA evidence implicates you"—he nodded toward Jamila—"they'll probably take this to a grand jury and seek an indictment for first-degree murder."

He paused and looked down. "Given what I've said—not to mention certain other circumstances—it's best we avoid that."

"What other circumstances?" I asked.

Mulrooney said nothing. I looked at Jamila. She wouldn't look back.

Was it because Jamila was black?

"Can't we move this case somewhere less …" I fumbled for the word. "Prejudicial?"

"I could ask the court. As you know, a change in venue would be at the court's discretion. No guarantees."

Mulrooney stared fixedly at his desk. "I hate to be the bearer of bad news, but you realize it is my job to prepare you for the worst."

I sighed. Jamila sat up straight. "So … what would my options be?" she said, looking braced for impact.

Mulrooney leaned on his forearms, hands clasped as if in supplication. "Of course, I'll do everything I can to dismiss any of their evidence or buy us time. I'll request the venue change. However, assuming the worst, the only sure way to avoid an indictment and trial is through a plea bargain. Most likely a plea to involuntary manslaughter based on diminished capacity."

I jumped up. "No. Way."

The elderly lawyer's gaze drifted my way. "I believe that's the client's decision."

"Jamila wants to be a judge. She's wanted that ever since law school. As long as I've known her. Do you realize what a guilty plea would do to her career?"

Mulrooney nodded, looking sad. "Yes."

"Then you have to know that's unacceptable."

I looked at Jamila for confirmation. She looked thunderstruck. "Surely," she said, in a near whisper. "It won't have to come to that."

"Let us hope not. However, you need to be ready for the possibility." Mulrooney's look bore into me. "The only other possibility is to come up with another suspect. I've made it clear to Conroy that he needs to treat this case as his first priority. We need to dig up something that'll blow their case out of the water."

I nodded, thinking, *I'll be damned if I rely on Conroy for that.*

φφφ

Before we left, Mulrooney advised Jamila to lay low and avoid talking to anyone else about the case without counsel present. "Let your attorneys handle everything," he said. Jamila concurred, but seemed to respond on autopilot.

As we drove back to the motel, I warned Jamila about the media's awareness of her situation. She only nodded and stared straight ahead.

"Jamila." I paused, considering my next words. "Is there something you're not telling me?"

She sighed. "Nothing important."

I wished I could believe her.

CHAPTER NINE

After dropping Jamila at the motel, I had to act. But where to start? The eyewitness. What was his name? Mulrooney hadn't said, and I'd neglected to ask. I called Mulrooney and left a message. Now what? Start with Billy Ray's friends. They knew about the confrontation. They also could've stolen the knife and clothes. They'd be the logical ones to frame Jamila. But who were they? And assuming I could track them down, what would I do? Torture them into confessing? Right.

Time was my enemy. The preliminary hearing was in two weeks. And Jamila's presentation was in three days. So I had only so much time to … what exactly? Exonerate Jamila? Do damage control?

I took a moment to think and try to pick a sensible course. Maybe I should start with the name I did know—Marshall Bower. Perhaps there was something to be learned from Billy Ray's stepfather, the man with all the local pull.

Sam McRae, girl of action, decided to find an Internet café. I figured it would take me all of five minutes to look him up.

The "café" turned out to be one lonely terminal tucked in the corner of a forlorn shop that sold cheap T-shirts in one of the strip malls a couple of miles north on Coastal

Highway. They charged an outrageous $20 for ten minutes. I figured I'd rather cough up the cash than run back to the condo, fetch Jamila's laptop and hunt around looking for free Wi-Fi.

As the connection—dial up, no less!—crept to life, I checked my watch. Almost 10:30. Okay, I had time. Still it was mere hours away from my meeting with Jinx. It felt like waiting to have a tooth pulled.

When the home page finally downloaded, I checked my favorite directory. Three listings for a Marshall Bower in Maryland. None of them in the area.

"Shit." Unlisted, no doubt. Given his apparent stature in the community, I guessed it was his way of avoiding contact with the hoi polloi.

I Googled the name, throwing in the terms "Eastern Shore" and "Ocean City." Results! Among the top hits was a blog post about Bower Farms, Inc. Bower, who reportedly owned amusement rides, arcades, a few hotels, and other real estate holdings, had diversified last year into the poultry business—big business on the Eastern Shore. His outfit was small compared to the heavy hitters like Perdue and Tyson, but according to the post dated two months ago, the company was making aggressive inroads into the industry. Enough to where it put the local farm and migrant worker protection groups on alert. The blog had been created by just such a group. The Farmworker Protection League, aka FPL. Interesting.

With another glance at my watch, I quickly Googled Bower Farms, Inc., for its address and phone number. A few more clicks and I had it mapped and printed on a dusty, but functioning ink jet printer.

With minutes to spare, I checked the blog for contact information. No phone number, just a gmail address. I went into my email and quickly shot off a message, expressing an interest in talking to someone at FPL about Bower Farms, and Marshall Bower and family, in particular. If Bower had the kind of clout that could end up railroading my best friend into pleading guilty to something she didn't do, I intended to find the guy's Achilles' heel.

In the meantime, I'd learn what I could on my own.

With address and map in hand, I went off in search of Bower Farms.

φφφ

Thirty minutes later, I was cooling my heels in the reception area decorated in soothing shades of red, yellow, black, and white. Soothing, that is, if you enjoy that particular riot of colors. Bower, for reasons known only to him and against all better judgment, had chosen to emphasize his loyalty to Maryland by doing up his office in the colors of the state's flag. A bit jarring to the eye and unlikely to win any awards from *Interior Design Magazine*.

Bower's receptionist, Gwen, a woman who looked to be in her early sixties with blonde hair piled high in a do that was (in an odd coincidence of sorts) fashionable during the early '60s, had told me Mr. Bower had a full schedule and was on a conference call at that time, but he might be able to "squeeze" me in if I waited. While waiting to be squeezed, I selected a magazine from the array on the ebony coffee table. *Poultry Today*. And the latest issue, too. How lucky can a girl get?

I was perusing one of the front-section department items ("Chicken Feed"—a gossip column for poultry farmers, if you can believe that), when I overheard Gwen say, "Oh, yes. All right." She paused and nodded with vigor, perhaps attempting to make the movement visible through the phone. "I understand. Yes. Okay. I'll tell her."

She placed the receiver in the cradle as gently as a jeweler placing a Faberge egg in a packing carton.

I leaned forward and bared my teeth in what I hoped resembled a winning smile. "I'm sorry, I couldn't help but overhear. Tell me what?"

Gwen's gaze flicked briefly to the desk blotter, then the wall over my shoulder, as if she were searching for the answer somewhere in the gaudy room.

"Let me guess. Mr. Bower won't be able to squeeze me in?"

"I … I'm afraid not." Gwen gave me a beseeching look.

"Perhaps I could schedule another time to meet him?"

"Well …" Her face contorted and she bit her lip. This was not looking good. "That may be complicated."

I took a deep breath. "Why is that?"

"Mr. Bower says he wants to have his lawyer present if he talks to you. I'd need to coordinate his schedule, as well." She sounded as perplexed as she looked. I felt almost the same. Almost.

I closed the magazine and, grinning with all I had, rose and said, "Tell you what. I'll call you later to set something up, okay? By the way, this is really great reading. Do you mind if I take it with me?"

φφφ

As I left Bower Farms' paean to all things Maryland, I reached a stunningly obvious conclusion: this is a small community. People talk to each other. They already know who I am and what I'm doing. It's going to be really hard to get any useful information from anyone. *That's why Conroy was hired. Duh!*

By heading directly for Marshall Bower, I had in effect thrown myself at a brick wall. Of course, I hadn't thought that a man who wasn't accused of anything would lawyer up. What was *that* all about?

When I returned to the motel, I found a note from Jamila saying she'd gone to the beach to relax and try to forget.

After a quick call to her cell phone (which she'd turned off or wasn't answering), I left a message about needing to use her laptop to do some research. Not waiting for a yea or nay on this issue, I took the laptop to the nearest coffee shop with Wi-Fi. I tried looking into Billy Ray Wesley's background, seeking anything that would point to another person or thing I could investigate about the man. Scanning the local news items, I ran across a really interesting tidbit.

About four months ago, the local paper had announced that Billy Ray was engaged to a Danielle Beranski. Danni, I thought. The quiet one who had hung back while the others followed their leader to the car after that first encounter.

The engagement must have been called off, since Danni was "no longer his girl," as I recalled. So, what was she doing hanging out with the guy? Maybe they'd decided to part as friends. Or maybe there was more to Danni than met the eye. Either way, she seemed like an excellent source of dirt on good old Billy Ray.

I looked up D. Beranski and found a local address and phone. After pinpointing her location on a map, I called the number (using *67 to shield my own) and got voice mail delivered in the shy girl's distinctly faltering tone. I disconnected without leaving a message and shut down the computer.

Surely, it wouldn't be stepping on Ellis Conroy's toes to have a short talk with Danni Beranski.

CHAPTER TEN

Danni Beranski lived in an old Victorian in Berlin (pronounced BER-lin, emphasis on the first syllable, unlike the German namesake), a small town only a few minutes drive from Ocean City. Its gingerbread brown with yellow trim had faded a bit with time and weather, but a realtor could still call it "quaint," as opposed to a "fabulous fixer-upper."

Climbing the creaky porch steps, I rang the doorbell and practiced smiling.

Eventually, a blonde woman in jeans and an oversized T-shirt opened up. She could have been Danni's mother, although she looked young for that.

"Hi. Is Danni here?"

She looked puzzled for a moment, then said, "And who are you?"

"I … met Danni recently. There was something we discussed and I was hoping to continue that discussion."

Still looking uncertain, she said, "Okay. Your name?"

"Sam McRae."

"Wait here, please," she said, as she turned and half closed the door on me. So far, so good.

When Danni opened the door, her eyes widened a moment. "Oh, hi," she said.

"Hi, Danni. I know we didn't meet under the best circumstances, but I hoped we could talk a little about your ex-boyfriend." The dead one. "Would that be okay?"

"Sure." Danni stepped outside and shut the door behind her. She gestured toward a porch swing and a sturdy rocking chair.

I sat in the rocker and took in the view of small-town America. The air was perfumed with a heady floral scent.

"This seems like a nice place to live," I lied through my teeth. The thought of living in a place so small everyone knew everyone else's business gave me the creeps.

"It's okay." Danni perched on the swing and twisted a strand of hair.

"Was that your mother I just met?"

"Oh, no. That's Jill. I rent one of her rooms."

"Just so you know, I'm helping my friend, Jamila, defend against any charges that she killed Billy Ray."

She nodded, looking off into the middle distance.

"I understand that you were once engaged to Billy Ray. Can I ask what happened?"

"He …" Her voice trailed off and she shook her head. "It just didn't work out."

"Did he call it off?"

"No. I did." She spoke with more conviction than I'd heard up to that point.

"If you don't mind my asking, why?"

She shook her head, mute. For a moment, I thought she was refusing to answer.

Finally, she said, "Things with him were too weird …."

"What do you mean?"

"He was into things that I didn't want to get involved with."

I nodded. Now, we were getting somewhere.

"What things?"

"Business stuff. I'm not sure exactly, but I think a lot of it wasn't on the up and up."

Now, we were *really* getting somewhere.

"Could any of those things have involved people who might want to kill him?"

Her expression distorted, and I thought she was going to cry, but instead she laughed. "Plenty of people might have wanted to kill him."

"Anyone specific?" I had to restrain myself from grabbing and shaking her.

"Not really."

"He seemed to have a lot of friends. You, for instance, remained friends?"

"Friends? Ha! People just used him. Why not? He was being groomed to take over his stepdaddy's business. Funny how many friends you make when you go from rags to riches."

If I hadn't been careful, my jaw might have dropped into my lap. "So, he wasn't always rich?"

"No." Her mouth pursed with distaste. "His mother was trailer trash who married Marshall Bower for his money. Everyone knows it."

"So everyone sucked up to him. Is that how it was?"

"Oh, yeah. And talk about a dysfunctional family." She raised her hands and slid off the porch swing onto her feet. "It was a horrible situation, and I didn't want to marry into that. On top of everything else …"

She stopped and looked at me. "Anything else you want to know?"

I pondered the question. *What about Junior?*

"You said Billy Ray was being groomed to take over the business. Why not Marshall Jr.?"

She chuckled. "Junior? Billy Ray can be a class-A jerk, but he has basic common sense. Junior doesn't have the business savvy Billy Ray does. Or did."

"So if Bower didn't trust Junior with the business, I take it Billy Ray was his only alternative?"

"We-e-ll." She stretched the word out. "There was Marsha, but she flew the coop ages ago."

"Marsha?"

"His daughter. She never got along with her dad, so she up and split. Hasn't been seen round these parts in forever. Like I said. Dysfunctional. Totally sad." She paused. "Anything else?"

"Actually, yes." I stood up. "Could you give me the names of everyone who was with Billy Ray the day my friend and I … first met him?"

She shrugged. "Sure. But I don't really think any of them killed him, to be honest."

"How can you be so sure?"

"Well … Billy Ray could be difficult. But now that he's dead, they've got no one to leech off." She frowned. "I guess I was really no better. I should've steered clear of him and his groupies after we called the wedding off." She waved a dismissive hand. "Doesn't matter now, does it?"

I removed a small notebook and pen from my shoulder bag. "So … those names?"

φφφ

Danni turned out to be the proverbial gold mine of information, providing not only the names of Billy Ray's groupies, but the address for Marshall Bower's happy home. There's nothing like love gone wrong to turn your average person into your very own confidential informant.

Armed with my list of names and the laptop, I headed toward the nearest coffee shop with free Wi-Fi and looked up the addresses. I suspected none of these sources would be terribly forthcoming, but I had to start somewhere. I figured I'd take my chances with Karla Dixon, the busty redhead.

Perhaps as a woman, I could more easily establish rapport with her.

Karla lived in a recently built condo in West Ocean City—across the bridge from Ocean City proper. I climbed the outdoor stairs that led to the second level of the sleek, blue and gray building and turned down the walkway to reach Unit #204.

A knock on the door and half a minute later, Karla opened up and greeted me with an open mouth and wide green eyes.

"Hi. I don't know if you remember me—"

"Yeah, I remember you. What do you want?" She crossed her arms.

Nice. A woman who got right to the point

"I'd like to talk to you about Billy Ray. But, first, I'd like to introduce myself. My name is Sam McRae and I'm—"

"I know what you're doing. Everyone does, okay? You're helping that awful lawyer Mulrooney with your friend's defense, right?"

"Yes, I was just about to explain—"

"Save your explanations. I loved Billy Ray and now he's dead." Her voice cracked on the last word. "Okay, so maybe he wasn't nice to your friend, but that was no reason to kill him." Her volume rose and her face reddened as she spoke. Her eyes actually teared up.

I cleared my throat. "My friend has been accused, but that doesn't make her guilty. I'm just trying to clarify—"

"Stop it! You're not trying to clarify anything. You're just looking to lay the blame on someone else. You're trying to confuse everyone. That's all you criminal lawyers are good for. You're awful. How can you even come here and question me? Billy Ray's dead and I'll never get to see him again. Thanks to your friend."

Then she broke down and started sobbing.

I was speechless for a long moment. Finally, I said, "I am truly sorry for your loss."

She backhanded the tears from her crimson face. Her expression twisted in fury, she said, “Give me a break. You don’t give a damn.”

With that, she slammed the door shut.

That went well.

CHAPTER ELEVEN

I am so screwed. How could I help Jamila, if no one in this wretched backwater would talk to me?

It was coming up on 12:30 and I was starving. I stopped at a roadside stand that sold crab cakes and soft-shell crab sandwiches. Have you ever had a soft-shell crab? Full of green stuff. Don't ask. I bought a crab cake on a roll.

I checked the time. The hour for meeting with Jinx was closing in. I directed myself toward the Route 50 bridge and tried to prepare for whatever she had in store for me.

The trip to Java on the Beach was quick but stimulating. Negotiating Coastal Highway traffic in early summer has that effect. The June bugs were out in abundance. They drove, bicycled and scootered their way through the throng, willy-nilly. The roar of glasspacks competed with hopped-up Harleys and bullet bikes. The ambient air was a stew of exhaust.

I turned onto the side street leading to the parking lot near the boardwalk—surviving a near miss with a boy on a moped who shot in front of me at the last second.

I found a space—miracle of miracles!—near the ramp leading to the boardwalk. From there, I plunged into a crowd of tourists. People wearing T-shirts bearing messages like,

"I'm with Stupid." The kind of thing that was new thirty years ago.

Java on the Beach was tucked between a gift shop and a video arcade. The place looked dead. I strolled in.

The small box of real estate contained a counter and a motley collection of round tables with chairs. The few customers sat silent or spoke in hushed tones.

I spotted Jinx against the far wall. When we made eye contact, she jumped up.

"Yoo hoo! Here I am."

I surveyed the tiny shop. "So I see."

I put in my order and waited for my coffee. Jinx sat at the table, watching me and looking ready to burst.

I took a seat opposite her and leaned on my forearms. "So. What is it we need to talk about?"

She gave me a look of sheer rapture, eyes aglow.

"Ray Mardovich," she said.

For a moment, I said nothing. Just waited.

Jinx smiled and waited, too.

I said, "What about him?"

Jinx leaned across the table. "I know what he did to you."

"What are you talking about?" I wasn't going down without a fight.

She placed a confidential hand on my arm. I wanted to shake it off, but chose to keep our meeting from becoming confrontational.

"He did the same thing to me." Her eyes revealed pain. Pain I could completely understand.

I smiled and faked a small laugh. "I'm still at a loss."

"Sam, please." It was as close to begging as I'd ever heard from Jinx's lips. "Don't insult my intelligence."

She paused, biting her lip. "I know Ray was seeing you. He was seeing me before he got involved with you."

It was June and we were sitting in a stuffy little café on the boardwalk. The ocean breeze had died and the place smelled like rotten fish. Even so, my insides turned to ice.

I swallowed and said, "How do you know this?"

"I have photos. I followed him to your place." She gave me a hard look. "There's even one of you two kissing on the stairs. See?"

She pulled out a digital camera and turned it on. In the viewfinder, I saw an image of the stairs leading up to my apartment. Ray and I stood on them, K-I-S-S-I-N-G.

Swell.

"Jinx," I said. "Let's get to the point, shall we? We aren't exactly best buds. And I don't think you invited me here for tea and sympathy."

She nodded. "You're right. Okay, look. Ray's all set to be installed as the president of the state bar association, right?"

"Uh huh."

"Don't you see? He doesn't deserve it."

"Oh, I don't know." This whole discussion was making me queasy.

"Are you going to let this womanizing creep climb the ladder of success? Don't you think we should say something to stop him?"

"You're saying 'we' as if you and I were some kind of team. Pretty ridiculous, given our history."

"Look." She averted her gaze, then refocused on me. "I know we haven't been the best of friends."

I snorted. "There's the understatement of the year. Maybe the decade."

"But," she continued, undaunted. "We've both been hurt by this man. I say we pool our forces and get some payback."

"Exactly what is it you want to do?"

"Expose him. Tell everyone what Ray did. We have the pictures to prove it."

Yeah. Pictures of me.

"Jinx, I suggest you do as I did. Forget about the asshole. Seeking revenge will only wreck your life."

"Sam. I'm doing this. With or without your help."

I sat and gawked at Jinx. She smiled like the cat that ate the canary.

"Figures," I said. "Leave it to you to resort to blackmail."

"I never—"

"Stop right there." I rose and held up my hand. "Now I'm asking you not to insult *my* intelligence, okay?"

"I only—"

"I said stop and I mean it." I hissed the words through clenched teeth and leaned in toward Jinx. She clammed up.

"Now, listen," I said. "I can't stop you, if you really want to do this. I have no control over your actions. But, please keep in mind you're hurting people needlessly. I don't know if that means anything to you, since you're so capable of hurting people to satisfy your own interests. Even so, I hope you'll consider what I've said.

"No matter what, understand this." I stopped and shook a finger in her face. "I will not be blackmailed. You can threaten all you want, but I will not knuckle under to your demands. And I will have no part of your scheme."

I turned and, over my shoulder, said, "Thanks for the coffee. This has been fun," as I walked away.

Jinx, who'd been mute throughout my mini-rant, finally said, "Wait. I have another proposition."

I stopped and shook my head. "Are you crazy? What could you possibly offer me?"

"Wouldn't you like to know?"

This I had to hear.

I strolled back and leaned upon my vacated chair. "Fine. What is it?"

"An exchange." Jinx's eyes narrowed. "Your good friend, Jamila's arrest has already made the news. Wouldn't it be nice to get the charges dismissed before things went any further? What if I could help you with that? Would you help me then?"

CHAPTER TWELVE

I stared at Jinx, wanting to say, "Yes, I'll do anything to help her." However, part of me wondered if it really included blackmailing and/or publicly humiliating someone. Including myself.

After taking a moment to consider my words, I said, "Assuming, I'm interested—and that's a big assumption—what kind of help could you offer? And, more to the point, how can I trust you to deliver?"

"My family has old ties around here. I can probably help pull some strings."

I sighed. "That's nice, but we've already got a local lawyer who doesn't need any help pulling strings. So unless your family is even more influential than our own politically connected lawyer, I doubt there's much you could do for me."

We shared a moment of silence as this sank in.

"Look, Jinx, this has been really interesting, but I have to go," I said. "Before I do, could you explain why you're so anxious to get me on board? You've got the pictures. Why do you need me?"

Jinx blinked up at me. "People like you, respect you. I thought if I acted alone, people would dismiss me. Maybe even claim I'd doctored the photos, you know? These days it's so easy to do that. I could end up sounding like … Paula Jones or Monica Lewinsky. I wanted this to come from both of us. It would give the allegations more credibility."

I wondered if I was hearing things. Had Jinx just paid me a compliment?

"Please," she said. "Just promise me you'll think it over."

Great. I could expose Ray's womanizing to help keep my best friend's career from getting flushed down the toilet, while turning myself into another Paula Jones. And in league with the Devil herself, no less.

I thought I'd gag swallowing my pride, but said, "I'll think it over. But that's all. And I'll need more than verbal assurance of your good faith."

I left before Jinx could see the anguish written all over my face.

φφφ

I needed to clear my head, so I took a brisk stroll down the boardwalk. The fresh tang of ocean breeze cleansed the coffee shop's rotten fish smell from my body. That and my increased inhalation rate. What started as a stroll turned into a march. I stomped while fuming over Jinx's threat—or was it a proposal?—and the fact that she had photos of me and Ray. The thickening crowd parted like the Red Sea before Moses. I think my speed and facial expression sent a signal to make way. Or else. Before I knew it, I'd reached Thrasher's French Fries stand, which meant I was nearing the end of the boardwalk. The tantalizing smell of potatoes cooked in peanut oil tickled my nostrils. I stopped and stood, a rock awash in a sea of people.

What are you doing? I was wasting time and the thought made me even angrier.

I turned and pounded the boards to where I'd parked.

φφφ

I started the car and joined the flow of Coastal Highway traffic. Was it safe to assume that Billy Ray's male friends—Curtis Little and Dwayne Sutterman—wouldn't give me the time of day? No, but I was pretty sure they wouldn't welcome me with open arms. I turned into a strip mall featuring a coffee shop that advertised Wi-Fi access.

I settled in with a cup of black coffee and fired up the laptop. After opening the browser, I checked my email. My inbox was crammed with messages—mostly junk I could read later—however, one of them caught my eye. Someone named Amber from the Farmworker Protection League had responded to my request for information.

The message read: *Feel free to come by our offices so we can talk.* The email had a phone number in the signature line.

I let out a breath and almost smiled. At last. One person in this burg willing to talk to me. Perhaps I'd unearth a lead.

I dug out my cell phone and dialed the number.

CHAPTER THIRTEEN

The Farmworker Protection League had offices in an old house in Salisbury. The house had been converted into offices not unlike my own in Laurel.

I entered a small reception area, outfitted in furnishings with utility utmost in mind. A small second-hand wooden reception desk greeted me. Multicolored metal file cabinets lined the far wall. To the right, a sofa covered in a faded red and white floral pattern provided visitors a place to cool their heels.

As I walked in, I glimpsed in profile a slim brunette, late twenty-something woman dressed by L.L. Bean in Capri pants and a striped T-shirt. Engrossed in searching through a filing cabinet drawer, she squatted and bent to her task.

"Amber Moore?" I asked.

She jumped and turned.

"I'm sorry," I said. "I didn't mean to startle you. I'm Sam McRae. We spoke earlier."

She smiled and rose. "Right. Come in, come in."

Amber ushered me into the office where she worked as a summer intern at FPL. She offered me coffee or water. I declined and explained my interest in Marshall Bower.

"Oh, he's an interesting character, all right. Let's talk."

Thank God, I thought.

"So, where'd you study law?" she asked.

"University of Maryland."

"I'll be starting my third year there this fall," she said. She indicated a guest chair, taking a seat in a matching one. "It's nice to meet a fellow Terp."

I couldn't help grinning. Could it get much better than this?

"How did you end up here?" I asked.

"Maryland has a great environmental law program. I got interested in agricultural practices—use of pesticides, runoff into the Bay—that kind of thing. So I sought out opportunities to work on those issues and found out about this internship. This makes my second summer at FPL. As I learned more about the agricultural industry, I became aware of a number of other issues. Things you wouldn't believe. Worker safety problems, immigration issues, and employees working eighty-hour weeks for peanuts. And their living conditions …" She shook her head. "Don't get me started."

I thought about doing just that, but chose for the moment to focus on Marshall Bower.

"What can you tell me about Bower Farms and its owner?"

"Well, Marshall Bower got into the poultry business only recently. The really big players, like Purdue and Allen's, are institutions around here. However, Bower has connections and … I think he may tend to cut corners a little to try to compete with the big guys."

"Cut corners how?"

Amber clasped her hands and planted her elbows on the armrests. "How much do you know about the poultry industry?"

"Not much."

She smiled. "Let me give you a little tutorial then. You may find it helpful.

"For the major players, the days of family chicken farming are long gone. Poultry companies rely on contractors—known as 'grow-out farmers'—to raise the chickens. These are high-volume operations that use cheap, nonunion labor. The farmers don't even own the chickens. It's the companies that provide the chickens, their feed, and anything else needed to care for them."

She paused, as if waiting for questions.

"So, we're talking big business?" I said.

"Huge. Poultry processors on the Delmarva Peninsula and in the South have virtually sewn up the market. These businesses dominate the local economy. Yet most of their workers aren't locals."

"Really?"

She nodded. "When the chickens are ready for slaughter, the company sends a crew of chicken catchers to round them up and bring them to the processing plant. Because the poultry industry no longer pays enough to attract local workers, they've come to rely on migrant workers—many of them Hispanic, many of them of dubious legality, immigration-wise."

She paused to let this sink in.

"Are you telling me Marshall Bower cuts corners by hiring illegal alien workers?"

"I'm not saying that he does," she said. "But it has been known to happen. Using undocumented workers cuts costs. And we've become aware of cases in which illegal workers have been injured or killed due to poor working conditions."

I wondered if there was a point to this discussion and was about to ask, when she resumed her spiel.

"Illegal workers are afraid to report health and safety violations, so it's hard to prove anything against their employers. I couldn't say for sure that Bower Farms has engaged in these practices. But given the cutthroat competition—um, no pun intended—I suspect they may have done so."

"Where does Marshall Bower's stepson fit into this picture?"

"According to my confidential sources, Billy Ray was being groomed to take Bower's place at the helm of his vast empire. Essentially, Marshall Bower was sharing a great deal of authority over the poultry company with his stepson. Theoretically, Billy Ray could step in at a moment's notice and take over the whole company in the event of his stepfather's demise."

"So, he would've known about any shady hiring practices? Or poor working conditions?"

Amber nodded. "Even if he didn't know, he'd certainly be held responsible for them."

Could any of the hapless workers have wanted to kill their employer? Was there any straw I could grasp in this? Especially when I considered my alternatives. Billy Ray's friends. Probably not forthcoming. Conroy. *What a guy.* And Jinx. *Shit.*

"I'd like to take a look at Marshall Bower's operation," I said. "Talk to some of his employees. Any chance of that?"

"I can probably arrange it with a man I know there. When would you want to do this?"

"As soon as possible." I attempted to not sound desperate.

"All right. I'll try to set this up and get back to you with the details." She looked somber. "And just so you know, the tour won't be easy or pleasant."

CHAPTER FOURTEEN

I drove back to our motel. Was taking a peek at Bower's processing plant a smart move or simply ridiculous? Getting an up-close look at his operation could be quite revealing. Or not. Worrisome, since time was running out and I couldn't afford to spin my wheels.

En route, my phone rang. I pulled over to the side of the road.

"The cops are done with the condo," Jamila said. "I checked us out of the motel and moved our stuff back."

Her voice sounded strange. "What's the matter?"

"You'll see soon enough."

When I arrived at the condo, I couldn't believe my eyes.

I didn't know for sure what I was looking at until I climbed upstairs and saw the mess. The front of the condo had been egged. Rotten eggs.

"Jesus." I was numb with disbelief. The air was putrid with sulfurous fumes. Gasping air through my mouth to avoid gagging, I unlocked the door and hustled inside.

Jamila sat in the living room, her arms crossed, staring at the TV.

"Jesus!" I said again. "When did that happen?"

"Sometime *after* the cops left, I assume." Jamila spoke without looking at me. "They left this, too."

She got up and handed me an eight-and-a-half-by-eleven sheet of white paper. On it, someone had printed, "Die screaming nigger bitch!!!!" It looked like the product of a standard laser printer.

Nice. I was all out of words.

"At least they didn't stick it on a rock and throw it through the window," Jamila said, with false cheerfulness.

"Have you called the police?" Talk about sounding idiotic.

"I've been sitting here for the last half-hour trying to figure out why I should. Who's going to care? What are they going to do? Nothing. We can't link this note to anyone. And, even if we could, all it would do is give the prosecution more reasons why I have an ax to grind or a motive to kill that guy."

She crossed her arms tighter and scowled.

"If it makes you feel any better, I think I've hooked up with someone who might help us." I told her about my meeting with Amber and her promise to let me tour the processing plant.

She looked appeased, but only slightly. "That's interesting, but how does it help me?"

Fair question, I thought. "It's just a hunch. Bear with me on this. Bower Farms is a small fish in a big pond. However, according to what I've read, the business has been growing by leaps and bounds. How do you suppose they've done that?"

She shrugged. "Knowing people. Greasing the wheels." She rubbed her fingers together in a way that suggested money could be changing hands.

"Could be that. Or there could be more."

"Such as?"

"What if Bower Farms was cutting costs on worker safety or hiring illegal aliens?"

Jamila snorted. "So, what else is new?"

"Well, I think OSHA and the INS might take a pretty dim view."

She narrowed her eyes. "What are you suggesting?"

I paused to gather my thoughts. "Let's suppose—hypothetically—that Bower Farms is hiring illegal aliens and making them work for slave wages in unsafe conditions. If Billy Ray is supposed to take over the business, he'd be fully aware of these practices. For all we know, he might have been involved in smuggling migrant workers."

Jamila nodded. "Hypothetically, sure. So you think there might be murder buried among these hypotheticals?"

"Exactly."

She blew out a breath. "I sure hope you stumble across something soon. Bad enough I could be asked to plea to a crime I didn't commit. The humiliation of being scratched from the program is more than I can bear."

I gaped. "Have they canceled your presentation?"

"Not yet, but it's just a matter of time. After all, I'm supposed to be speaking on ethics. In three days."

I know. I read the program, too.

"I realize it seems like a longshot, Jamila, but Amber is the closest I've come to finding an ally." I kept mum about my meeting with Jinx. "It's at least worth a visit to a Bower Farms facility."

Jamila grunted and shrugged assent.

"Besides," I added. "Your arrest hit the papers early. Most of the attendees haven't even arrived."

"Right. Well, now they're arriving and calling me."

"Oh, no."

Her lips twisted in a grimace. "Oh, yes. Why do you think I've turned this off?" She pointed to her cell phone on the side table. "I don't even want to think about how many messages I have or who they're from."

I thought of the partners at her firm. This news couldn't be buying her any good will with them.

The creak of the front screen door and a brisk knock turned our heads.

"Who could that be?" I muttered.

I crept up to the door and checked the peephole. A well-groomed woman loomed into view, lips puckered, nose wrinkled. Behind her, a man stood, holding something on his shoulder. Apparently the rotten egg stench wasn't putting them off.

"Good grief," I whispered.

"What?"

I put my finger to my lips and padded away from the door. "I'm not sure, but I think there's a reporter out there," I said. "With a cameraman."

Jamila threw her hands up and fell back against the sofa. "Wonderful. What next?"

"Have you told anyone where we're staying?" I asked.

"I told Rudy, of course." Her husband was a man sensible enough not to talk to the press.

"I haven't told anyone." Then I thought of the rotten eggs.

Jamila must have read my mind. "I think we know who told them."

The knocking resumed. Would I have to act as Jamila's press agent now?

CHAPTER FIFTEEN

I peered through the peephole until the reporter and her sidekick left. Moving to the front window, I watched the two head for an unmarked van that gave no clue who they worked for. Awesome. The man stowed his camera in the back, as the woman—well-coifed reddish-brown hair, late twenties, medium build—slid into the passenger seat, clutching her notepad and pen.

I snorted. "I don't believe this. They have to know you won't be willing to discuss the case." Shaking my head, I added, "Journalists. They're goddamned vultures. Idiots and vultures."

Jamila remained silent, gaze fixed on the television. She'd muted the sound, but kept staring at the images. She was either inwardly steaming or taking this remarkably well.

"I guess those guys go after anything that even smells like a scoop around here," I said. "It must get old covering the farm beat and whatever rinky-dink occurrence passes for news in these parts." I knew how feeble and stupid I sounded, but I couldn't shake the feeling that Jamila was holding back.

"I'm not sure what else to do, except get a look at Bower Farms from the inside and hope it reveals something compromising. Maybe follow up with those guys who hung around Billy Ray." I prattled on like a moron, dancing around the point in a manner wholly unlike me.

"Jamila," I finally said. "Why did Mulrooney ask if you could think of a motive to kill Billy Ray?"

She heaved a sigh. "It's … nothing, really."

I steeled myself. *Jamila knows I have to ask.* "Are you positive?"

"Yes."

She cast a sad glance my way. One that seemed to belie her words.

Mulrooney had advised me to let Jamila choose whether to tell me about this, and he was in charge of this case. I couldn't force her to talk, so I simply had to leave it at that.

φφφ

Since Jamila seemed too numb to act, I took the initiative and scared up a watering hose from beneath the landscaped shrubbery around the building. A bit of digging through the junk drawer produced an adapter that let me attach the hose to the kitchen faucet. About a half hour later, I'd finished blasting rotten egg off the front porch and replaced the hose where I'd found it.

I washed up and was drying my hands when my cell phone rang. It was Amber.

"Up for a tour of the processing plant tonight?" she asked.

"Absolutely."

We arranged to meet at a mutually convenient spot on Route 50, where Amber would provide a ride to the plant. "My advice," she said, "don't eat beforehand."

φφφ

I had a few hours to kill, so I decided to confront the two men who'd been with Billy Ray on the day of our auspicious meeting. For Jamila to be set up, one of the people who'd been there that day had to be involved. Even if they only slammed the door in my face, I had to at least try to question them.

I took the laptop to the closest place with Wi-Fi to do a bit of Internet research on the men so I'd have an idea who I was dealing with. The names of the players were Curtis Little and Dwayne Sutterman. For kicks, I checked the Maryland Judiciary Case Search, which had docket information about civil, criminal, and traffic cases throughout the state.

Dwayne Sutterman's record wasn't spotless. I checked the entries. Nabbed a couple of times for possession and use. Each time he managed to get off with probation before judgment—a slap on the wrist. Luck? Or more? I searched for Curtis Little, but found nothing in the official docket. Which didn't mean he hadn't done anything. He just hadn't been caught.

I finished my research, packed up my things, and headed out to Curtis Little's place. The address I found for him was in a trailer park outside Berlin—a forlorn cluster of mobile homes on a large dirt lot behind a line of trees. The frontage was a carpet of weeds with a long, straight gravel driveway striped across it.

As my car crunched up the driveway, my expectations—already low—sank even further upon surveying my surroundings. I suspected the trailer park was well populated with people who didn't care for lawyers. No doubt, Curtis Little would have little incentive to answer my questions.

I located the trailer—a double-wide with a small porch—and knocked on the door. I vaguely recalled that Danni had mentioned in passing that Little was probably Billy Ray's best friend.

The door was pulled open by a chubby dark-complected young woman who looked up at me with liquid brown eyes. The top of her head barely reached my shoulders.

"Is Curtis Little here?"

She stared at me for a moment. Then, she began to rattle off Spanish.

My Spanish was more than a bit rusty, but I tried it out. "Por favor. Curtis Little aqui?"

She shook her head. "No," she answered in perfect Spanish, followed by an overwhelming flood of more of the same. I waved my hands to silence her.

"Lo siento. No hablo español. Un poco solamente. Muy, muy poco."

"Ah." She smiled and nodded. The woman spread her hands, looking helpless. "No hablo inglés. Um … sorry?" Her smile widened.

I returned the smile and nodded. "Uh … ¿Dónde está Curtis?"

She took a moment, no doubt trying to process Spanish thoughts into words I could understand. Finally, she dredged up, "He go. Doo-ah-ee-nay."

"He go" I got, but I wasn't quite sure what to make of that last part.

"So, Curtis has gone?" I waved my hands as I spoke, hoping to pantomime my message. "He left here—¿Vaya de aqui? And—¿Dónde está?"

I knew I wasn't getting all the words right, but she nodded throughout my performance like a pleased critic. When I asked my last question, she simply repeated, "Doo-ah-ee-nay," stretching out each syllable like warm taffy.

Is there a place called Dooaheenay? Never heard of it.

Then I realized I was an idiot.

"Do you mean his friend—um, amigo, Dwayne?"

Her smile would've lit up a subterranean cavern. "Sí, sí. Doo-ah-ee-nay."

"Well, thank you, um, gracias. I'll go see him. By the way, who are you? I mean, ¿Cómo se llama?" I held up a finger before she answered, retrieved a card from my shoulder bag, and handed it to her. "Me llamo Sam McRae," I said, running my finger under my name on the card as I did.

She spouted a few more words my stellar American public school education hadn't fully prepared me to understand, then added, "Me llamo Carmen Morales."

"Uh … su nombre es muy bonita, Carmen." God, I was shameless.

She blushed. "Muchas gracias."

"Well, nice to meet you. And, buenas tardes."

Even if she didn't understand all the words, her beaming expression indicated my intent was clear.

We smiled and nodded at each other a few more times before she finally closed the door.

CHAPTER SIXTEEN

I headed farther west on Route 50 to Dwayne Sutterman's place. On the way, I passed a flatbed truck laden with crated chickens. The odor suggested an overflowing septic tank on wheels. Upon closer inspection, I could see the chickens crammed so tightly their feathers fluttered between the slats like tiny flags of surrender.

"Poor birdies," I muttered, as I slowed to turn off the highway. The truck zoomed on, its driver heedless of me or his passengers.

The Glades apartment complex was a step up from Curtis's trailer park home. Part of it might survive if a tornado ripped through the area. The apartments were organized into four-story units of light brown brick with beige trim. I strolled the grounds of manicured grass, lined with boxwood shrubs and the occasional bed of daylilies and impatiens, until I located Dwayne Sutterman's building. It was only early June, but the summer heat was already creeping in. A trickle of sweat inched down my spine as I climbed to the top floor. I knocked at his door and waited.

I could hear a rustling sound within. Several thumps and a few mumbled words later, a man opened up. I recognized him from our first encounter with Billy Ray.

"Yeah." A toothpick hung from the corner of his mouth. Although his flint-gray eyes were unfocused, his gaze traveled up and down my body, like a scanner.

"Hi, Dwayne. You may remember me from a few days ago in the parking lot with Billy Ray."

"Uh huh. You want something or what?"

The pungent odor of pine-scented air freshener drifted from inside the apartment. Beneath that scent, I detected the unmistakably skunky scent of weed. Unless I missed my guess, Dwayne's eyes weren't the only thing unfocused about him.

"I'd like to talk to you and Curtis, if I could."

Dwayne said nothing. His gaze drifted to my face and stayed there.

"Uh, Dwayne. Is Curtis here?"

More silent staring.

I waved my hand before his eyes. "Hello? Anyone home?"

Dwayne's expression crumpled into one of annoyance. He grabbed my hand and cocked it back at the wrist. I sucked my breath in hard, as pain shot from my wrist to my elbow.

Keeping a hard grip on my hand, Dwayne leaned close, his face hovering inches from mine. "Don't fuckin' do that," he growled, enunciating each word so slowly, minutes seemed to elapse between them. "Do you understand?"

"Sure, sure," I gasped. "Sorry."

"Good." He pushed me and I stumbled backwards to the top of the stairs. Only good balance and quick reflexes prevented my tumbling down them.

"Are you going to tell me what you want?" His voice was as sour as his expression. *If this guy is stoned, I'm sure ruining his buzz.*

I sighed. "First, I'd like to know if Curtis Little is here." I was starting to feel like a damned parrot.

"No. Is that it?"

"I'll settle for you then. Who were you talking to just before you opened the door?"

"And how is that any of your goddamned business?"

"Is there anyone else here?"

Dwayne pressed his lips together and shook his head.

"Right," I said. "Then let's talk about Billy Ray."

"What's there to say? Your nigger friend killed him."

"How can you be so sure?"

"All the evidence points to her, doesn't it?"

"Not really."

"Oh, yes it does. What about the knife? What about the comb?"

What about the fact that you know all this?

"It's interesting you should bring those things up. I don't think the police have shared any of that information with the press." I paused to watch the effect of these words. He just looked surly. "In fact, cops tend to be very close-mouthed about evidence in ongoing investigations. So unless you have an inside source, I can't imagine how you'd know about the knife and the comb."

Dwayne's lips curled back in disdainful amusement.

"My brother is a detective. He's working a homicide. Three guesses which case he's just been assigned to."

For a moment, I was lost for words. The nepotism and cronyism in these parts was stunning.

"That's interesting. I wonder how your brother the cop would feel about your pot-smoking habit?"

"Yeah, right. I don't have a habit. You can't prove anything. Besides, he's a homicide detective, not a narc, you stupid bitch."

Dwayne snickered, then chuckled. This built into laughter. He reached into his pocket, pulled out a used tissue and blew his nose. A slip of paper came out and drifted to the doormat unnoticed.

I stooped to pick up the piece of paper. It read: "Maria Benitez" with a long string of numbers beneath it.

Dwayne stopped laughing. He snatched the paper from my hand, retreated inside, and slammed the door.

CHAPTER SEVENTEEN

Maria Benitez? Who the hell was that? Googling the name could produce ten million hits easily. I wished I had a photographic memory for numbers. I pulled into the 7-Eleven parking lot. Amber waited in her burnt-orange Prius, sipping a coffee. I pulled my convertible top up and grabbed a cup of brew before I joined her.

"Get ready," she said, as she turned the ignition.

"Dare I ask for what?"

"Some pretty harsh realities." Amber's lips twisted briefly. She backed out and drove off.

We rolled past flat fields of soybeans—according to Amber—stretching out in green rows toward a horizon punctuated with trees and a few houses.

"Soybeans are among the most important crops in this region," Amber explained.

"Why?"

"They have many uses. They feed people and livestock, for one thing." Amber paused, taking the time to check before passing a slow-moving farm vehicle. The operator even pulled to the side of the road for her. I marveled at this simple politeness that was so conspicuously absent at home.

"The Eastern Shore is the most concentrated agricultural area in Maryland," she continued, after passing the vehicle. "It makes up nearly a third of Maryland's agricultural land and produces more than half its major crops, like corn, soybean, wheat, and barley."

"You're a regular agricultural encyclopedia."

Amber laughed. "Sorry if I sound like an ad for the Chamber of Commerce. This place and subject have become my life. I don't get to talk to many people about it."

"How about your coworkers at the FPL?"

Amber frowned. "We're running out of those. The FPL has had to cut paid staff. We rely almost exclusively on volunteers and workers funded by grants."

"Is that how your internship works?"

"Yes. It's paid by a grant from the Chesapeake Bay Foundation. Unfortunately, that grant only stretches so far."

I pondered how lonely she must get in that little house in Salisbury. Especially as the only law student, probably eager to talk to someone with similar interests.

My thoughts were interrupted by an overpowering smell.

"Yeesh!" I said, flapping my hand. "Someone's been fertilizing their fields."

"Get used to it. That smell just means we're getting close to the plant."

"You mean …?"

"Yeah." She turned toward me with a wry smile. "It just gets worse."

φφφ

We pulled up at the processing plant, a low flat-roofed warehouse-like building, and left the car in the small dirt lot. A short brown man hustled out to greet us. He wore a pair of plastic boots and a slicker. A paper filter swung from an elastic cord around his neck. I focused hard on not succumbing to dry heaves from the overwhelming stench.

"¡Hola, Señorita!" our greeter said, smiling and nodding.

"Hola, Manuel. Ésta es mi amiga, Sam McRae."

"Uh … hola, Manuel." I extended a hand and he grabbed and shook it, grinning hugely.

"We're taking a tour." Amber gestured that we'd be going inside. "Okay?"

"Sí, sí. Tour? Uno momento."

Manuel disappeared into the building.

"Just getting some protective gear for us," Amber explained.

I nodded. *To protect us from what?*

Our host reemerged with plastic gear similar to his and masks for each of us. After I'd snapped my filter into place, Amber eyed me.

"Ready?" she said, her voice muffled.

Behind the mask, I grimaced. "As I'll ever be."

Inside, the plant was dimly lit with blue lighting. It took a moment for my vision to adjust. My ears were assaulted, however, with a cacophony of squawking.

"The low lighting is supposed to calm the birds," Amber explained.

"Tell that to the birds," I muttered.

Once my vision had adjusted, my first view was of pails. White plastic pails filled with dead chickens.

I swallowed hard, not only to hold back revulsion but because the stench within the building had a formaldehyde-like bite. The bile rising in my throat wasn't helping matters.

Across the room, I spotted plastic crates full of live chickens. Several workers—mostly women, their faces obscured with strapped on breathing filters—pulled chickens out by their legs in clumps and walked them to two long conveyors. They hung the hapless birds, flapping, by their feet.

"Those conveyors …" I said, unable to finish.

"Take them to slaughter," Amber said, her tone matter-of-fact. "Do you want to take a closer look?" She sounded solicitous. My eyes must have betrayed my queasiness and disgust.

I swallowed bile. "Yes." I had an opportunity to see how Bower Farms worked from the inside. I didn't want to blow that. So I needed to see what went on, no matter how horrible. The mask wasn't cutting it, but it would have to do.

The mesh platform we trod provided little protection from the unidentifiable liquid sloshing around the floor. I tried to avoid thinking about what it was.

I've always prided myself on being able to stare ugliness in the face and survive. But when I saw those frantic, thrashing chickens being dipped into a tub of water, then jolted with electric shocks—to stun them, Amber said, and make the slaughter "more humane"—I thought I'd lose it. I chomped on my lip so hard, I nearly broke the skin. I thought of birthday cakes and happy kittens to keep from blubbering like a baby.

To distract myself further, I forced myself to converse. "How come it smells so bad?" I croaked.

"The combination of blood, chicken fat, manure, and uric acid makes for a nice brew, doesn't it?" Amber quipped.

I flashed back to every time I'd had chicken soup when I was sick. I nearly threw up in my mask. *Never again!*

For a moment, the fumes, the lines of chickens headed toward decapitation, and my thoughts threatened to overwhelm me. I staggered to the wall and reached out for support. My fingers touched stickiness and I yanked them back.

"What the hell?" I said.

"Oh, shit." Amber took my arm and ushered me to a wash basin. "Here you go. Rinse up and I'll scrounge up some gloves." Her voice sounded far away, muffled beneath the mask.

"What was that?"

Amber's eyes—her only visible feature above the mask—fixed on me. "You don't want to know."

I grabbed the soap and washed my hands—scrubbing hard, rinsing, and repeating five times.

While Amber went in search of gloves, I watched the women in their repetitive task. My sight had adjusted enough to make out their features—light brown skin and dark eyes, looking impassive above white masks. Chicken-bearing automatons in an endless cycle of grabbing and hanging frightened birds.

I felt like I was in the world's worst sci-fi B movie ever. Like *Soylent Green* with chickens.

But it's okay to eat chickens, isn't it? That's what I kept telling myself. But those poor, helpless birds ....

I turned away and leaned against the sink, swallowing and blinking back tears. I couldn't look another minute.

Amber appeared at my elbow, offering the gloves.

"I'm sorry," I said, sniffling and wiping my eyes. I steeled myself. "Could we take a break?"

Her eyes softened. Placing a hand on my arm, she said, "Sure. Don't worry about it."

CHAPTER EIGHTEEN

Once I'd escaped from the dark confines of the plant, I ripped the mask off and gulped air.

"Jesus." I leaned over at the waist and planted a hand on each knee, trying to regain my bearings.

I could feel Amber approach from behind.

"That was … even worse than I imagined."

"Yeah. It is kind of gross."

I took a last deep breath and managed to straighten up. "I'm sorry. I feel like such a …" I struggled to say the word. The one I had in mind was "wuss."

"Don't worry about it. Honestly. You aren't the only one to react this way."

"Really?"

She nodded. "I've brought other aspiring legal interns here. They come with the best of intentions and lots of glowing hopes of doing the right thing."

"I'll bet." I thought of my own initiation into the world of the public defender so many years ago. What a bright-eyed naïve little person I'd been, even after spending part of a hard childhood in Bed-Stuy.

She grinned. "Hey, you made it to the electric stunner. Some can't even make it through the door."

Her warmth and support emboldened me. I managed a smile. "I guess that makes me a Rambo by comparison."

Despite her assurances, I was rethinking the visit. Desperation had prompted it, but I wasn't sure how much I could gain from it. However, while I was there, I asked Amber if I could speak to one or two of the workers.

As Manuel wandered by, Amber caught his attention and communicated my thoughts. She spoke much better Spanish than I, though she still stumbled over a few words now and then. Manuel nodded and hustled off.

"He's going to look for a couple of workers," she said. "I can probably translate most of what they say."

φφφ

A short brown-skinned woman with luminous dark eyes and raven hair approached me cautiously—the way a wild stallion might approach a horse trainer. Manuel had a hand on her shoulder. It almost looked like he was herding her toward me.

Manuel introduced the woman as Conchita Ruiz and launched into rapid Spanish patter. "He's telling her your name and that you're not a cop or immigration," Amber explained.

I nodded. Conchita's face relaxed, but only a little.

"Hola, Conchita," I said, trying to sound friendly. "Where are you from? What country?"

I waited while Amber translated. Conchita responded with a few quick words that flew by me, but I picked up the word "Honduras."

"She says hello, it's nice to meet you, and she's from Honduras," Amber said.

I nodded and smiled. *Well, at least I understood one word.*

"Conchita, how did you get here?"

Amber translated my question. Conchita's face froze. For a moment, I thought she'd bolt.

Amber said a few more words in a reassuring tone. Conchita seemed somewhat, if not entirely, appeased. She spit out a whole slew of words I had no hope of understanding. Amber nodded, interrupting now and then, as if for clarification. When they'd finished their exchange, Amber turned to me.

"She says she came here by train, paid for by relatives. I asked which connecting bus line brought her here, because you know there aren't any train stations on the Eastern Shore. She claimed she couldn't remember." Amber paused and added. "Frankly, I think she's lying. If I had to guess, she was probably brought here in the back of a panel truck. With a whole lot of other immigrant workers."

"So, she's probably illegal."

Amber looked somber. "I'd put money on it."

This came under the heading of interesting information. If Billy Ray were in charge of hiring plant workers, he'd have to know many of them were illegal immigrants. Possibly even arranged for them to be brought in.

Which raised another interesting question. Could Billy Ray's murder pertain to that? Or could it pertain to other illegal activities his friends engaged in? Like the "pot-free" Dwayne Sutterman and Curtis Little? After all, workers weren't the only things that got illegally smuggled across the border. This could merit some additional research on my part.

φφφ

After trying to squeeze a bit more information from Conchita and a couple of other workers and getting little for my efforts, Amber drove me back to my car.

"Even if you're not with INS, they're afraid of strangers," she said.

"Who can blame them?" I understood their lack of trust for any authority, especially around here. I felt it down to my bones.

Amber pulled her car up beside mine, threw it into "park" and sighed. "These people." She shook her head. "They're underpaid and work in the worst sort of conditions. Yet, they're afraid to complain for obvious reasons. It's a vicious cycle."

She gazed at me. "Has any of this helped?"

"If nothing else, it's given me food for thought."

She looked quizzical. "How so?"

"Nothing solid. Just random thoughts at this point."

"What do you think you'll do?"

I paused before answering. I wasn't sure how much to share. *And why was she asking?*

"I'll just keep looking around and talking to people." A suitably vague answer that seemed to satisfy her.

"Well, if there's anything else I can do for you, feel free to call," Amber said. She pulled a card and a pen from her shoulder bag. "Here's my cell number. You can reach me on it anytime."

φφφ

As I drove away, my thoughts returned to Curtis Little. Who was the Spanish-speaking woman who answered his door?

Curtis was supposed to be Billy Ray's closest friend. Perhaps he'd worked as an unofficial recruiter for Bower Farms. Could he also be working with Dwayne Sutterman, smuggling drugs from south of the border along with farm workers?

If Curtis and Billy Ray had a falling out, it could have jeopardized their illegal activities. These things happened all the time. One bad guy would turn against the other. The possibility of blackmail or extortion was ever present in such relationships. So much for honor among thieves.

These scenarios were only possibilities, but ones I needed to explore.

φφφ

I ran by Curtis's trailer again, but no one answered my knock. It was getting late and I was tired. I decided to call it a day.

As I left the trailer park, I heard an old car cough to life. I turned onto the highway and headed for Ocean City as a beat-up green Chevy lumbered onto the road behind me.

Dusk was setting in and headlights were snapping on. The Chevy's headlights shone at odd angles, making the car look walleyed. It made no move to overtake me. Nor did it lose distance. It stayed roughly three car lengths behind me.

As I hit the traffic waiting at the Route 50 drawbridge, I saw the car was still back there. The darkened windows allowed no view inside.

"Coincidence?" I muttered. "Probably." Lots of people took Route 50 into town everyday. Even so, my heart hammered.

Traffic started moving. After we'd crossed the bridge, I turned right and glanced in the rear view mirror. The green Chevy followed.

I hung a quick left down a side street. An impulsive move, but a good test. At first, I thought I'd lost him. "Silly," I said, shaking my head. Then, the car appeared in my mirror again.

When I reached the highway, I hung another left, then immediately pulled into a parking lot and tucked the car in behind a building with a high fence shielding it from the side road. I waited and watched, hoping they wouldn't catch on.

The Chevy passed by the entrance I'd taken. They had no clue what I'd done. Either that or I was imagining things.

I realized I was holding my breath and exhaled with relief. I took a moment to close my eyes and relax my shoulders, which were grazing my earlobes.

CHAPTER NINETEEN

I sat in the shadows, recovering my composure. Was I being ridiculous? Or had I been followed?

My phone jangled to life. My eyes snapped open, and my head nearly hit the ceiling.

The caller ID said it was Jinx. Ignore or take?

The phone rang again. Finally, I answered.

"Yes, Jinx."

"Have you decided?"

"Fine, thank you. How are you?"

"Waiting to hear back." Jinx sounded annoyed. She didn't seem to get the joke. What a surprise.

"That's because I haven't made a decision."

A long dramatic pause. The kind babies make before they start screaming. To Jinx's credit, she didn't.

"You have until Friday night. No later."

"Why Friday?"

"Because Ray gets installed on Saturday night at the banquet, and I need to know if you'll be with me or not."

Two days?

"I still need more than your verbal assurance that you'll keep your end of the bargain, if I do this," I said.

"You'll get it. But I need to know where you stand before midnight on Friday."

She hung up.

Just as I closed the phone, it rang again. This time it was Mulrooney. Despite the slight shake in my hand, I managed to flip the phone open and answer the call.

"Mulrooney here," he said in response to my greeting. "How's it going?"

Lousy. I wanted to say it, but that would be so wrong.

I gave him a brief rundown of my day.

"Hmm. I'm afraid I'm not surprised. I hope Conroy is getting somewhere."

I wouldn't want to pin my hopes on that, I thought. "I wondered, could you give me the name of the eyewitness? I'd really like to talk to this person."

"No problem. His name is Roger Powers. I even have an address."

Fishing through my shoulder bag, I managed to find my notebook and pen. I took down the information and thanked Mulrooney before hanging up. Powers lived right up the road from our condo on Bayview Drive. I sat in the growing gloom for a moment and thought about what I'd ask him before starting the car.

I slipped back onto Coastal Highway. As I drove, I mentally reviewed the questions I intended to ask Powers: what were you doing out that night? Where were you going? Where were you coming from? Do you wear glasses? Etc., etc. Meanwhile, wild speculations about Billy Ray's possible connections to drug smuggling and trafficking in illegal alien workers ran in a continuous loop through the back of my mind.

As I turned onto Bayview Drive and headed toward the Powers address, my phone rang. I pulled over to check the ID. The number was unfamiliar. I answered anyway.

"Hello?"

"Ms. McRae?" The voice was a low murmur.

"Yes."

"You need to come to Bower Farms plant. Right now."

"Who is this?"

"Never mind that. There's someone you need to see."

"Wait. I'm not going there in the middle of the night, all by myself. Sorry."

"Did you want to see Curtis Little?"

I paused. "Who is this?"

"A friend."

"Yeah, I'll bet. This is a blast, but I'm tired and I don't have time for games—"

"Neither do I. And neither does Curtis." The voice turned acidic.

"Then tell him to get his ass over here to see me or meet me at a decent hour. Or better still, ask him to call me himself. Thanks."

I hung up, stared at the phone and shook my head. I'd set it aside and started driving when it rang again. The caller ID showed the same number.

I flipped it open. "Hello, is this Curtis's good friend again?"

"Come to Bower Farms," the caller intoned, "if you want to see Curtis Little alive."

This time the caller hung up on me.

CHAPTER TWENTY

After calling Jamila to tell her not to wait up for me, I got on the phone to Amber Moore to get the exact address. Then I called 911 and told them about the call. I turned the car around and headed back toward the processing plant, wondering who or what I'd find. As for Jamila, I figured the less she knew, the better.

When I arrived on the scene, the lot where we'd parked mere hours earlier was overflowing with cars. Many of them sported rooftop visibars, creating a red-and-blue disco scene. Uniformed cops swarmed the grounds. One stood at the door, apparently on guard.

I walked up to the cop on guard. "What's happening?"

He looked at me. "Who are you?"

"I'm Sam McRae. I was the one who got the phone calls."

I won't say his jaw dropped, but his eyes betrayed shock. "The detective will want to talk to you," he said, his voice much calmer than he looked.

Great. I waited as the young man spoke into a walkie-talkie, then turned back to me and said, "He'll be here in a moment."

I smiled. "Thank you." I think.

The door opened and a man with a face cut from granite emerged. He stood roughly an inch shorter than me, but looked solid. His hair was dark and wavy, with ripples of gray threading through it.

"Detective Amos Morgan," he said without preamble. His arm extended and I grasped a hand as hard and calloused as a cowboy's.

"Sam McRae."

"Tell me about these phone calls."

I did so, as he scribbled in a small spiral notepad.

"Would you recognize this Curtis Little if you saw him?"

I thought back, trying to picture the guy in the lot who wasn't Billy Ray or Dwayne.

"Maybe," was about the best I could do.

"Come with me."

We entered the building. The lights were on, eerie as I remembered them. The equipment must have been hosed down because it looked clean. The walls, however, still looked sticky. The floors still wet.

Detective Morgan and I picked our way toward a dark shape forming in the gloom. A couple of jumpsuited technicians were setting up lights, as if for a photography shoot. As we drew close, the lights snapped on.

I sucked in a breath. I remembered the face. Curtis Little. He slumped from one of the hooks used to move the chickens down the conveyor.

"Is that him?" Morgan prompted.

"Uh huh."

Little's face was sheet white in the glare of the lamps. His heavy-lidded eyes expressionless.

"How …?" My voice trailed off.

"Stabbed in the gut." Morgan pointed toward Little's abdomen with his pen. The lower part of the dark shirt he wore was wet. A bloodstain.

φφφ

"So what was your connection to Little?" Morgan asked for the fifth or sixth time. We sat in his car at the scene. He asked questions and took lots of notes.

"I told you, Little was with Billy Ray the day he harassed me and Jamila Williams. I've been trying to touch base with him without success. Frankly, getting people to talk to me has been hard. The phone calls were weird to say the least."

"Did you perceive Little as a threat?"

"Are you kidding? Of course not."

"Even though those calls were from his phone?"

"Like I said, I didn't recognize the number. Or the voice."

"What about your friend?"

"My friend knows nothing about this. Nothing."

Morgan gave me his best cop stare. I had no more to say.

"You realize you may have been the last one to talk to him?" he said.

"Other than the killer," I added.

He smirked. "Right."

My stomach clenched. *Why did he sound so sarcastic?*

φφφ

By the time Morgan cut me loose, it was in the early hours of Thursday morning. Too late, I supposed, to talk to the eyewitness. Maybe. Just for kicks, when I got to Bayview Drive, I passed the condo and checked the address. To my surprise, lights were on inside the place. Almost every window. You'd have thought it was early evening instead of the wee hours. Maybe Roger Powers was a night worker. That would explain his presence so late at the scene of Billy Ray's murder.

I pulled up to the curb and cut the engine. Silence descended. Not even gulls were crying. Traffic noise was muted. Only the rhythmic swish of water on nearby bulkheads was audible. It felt like I had cotton in my ears.

I exited the car and proceeded up the driveway to a curved walkway leading to the rambler's front door. The porch light was on. A party? Midweek? When I reached the door, I heard the faint sound of music. Classical? I knocked, tentatively.

I glanced at my watch. 2 A.M. *Good grief.* Powers was either a night worker or a serious insomniac.

The door opened up. A tall young man in his mid to late twenties with short dark hair and a faintly distracted look opened up. "Can I help you?" he asked, blinking.

For a moment, I simply froze. It was 2:00 in the morning, and I was questioning an eyewitness who claimed to have seen my best friend at the scene of a murder. *What should I ask him? Why isn't my brain working? Maybe because it's 2 A.M. Duh!*

I snapped out of my reverie. "Hi. I couldn't help noticing you were up. My name is Sam McRae and I'm an attorney representing the suspect in the murder that took place down the street. Would you have time to answer a few questions?"

He nodded and said, "Sure. C'mon in."

I breathed a sigh. *Now, how hard was that?*

φφφ

Ten minutes later, I'd learned that Roger Powers was a musician. This explained the nocturnal schedule. Powers was in a band that played regular gigs around town. A variety of oldies and album rock. Anything from the late '60s up to the early '90s.

Powers offered coffee, which I gratefully accepted. I drank my way through three cups and endured a mind-numbing exchange of polite chitchat to warm him up for my laundry list of questions.

Me: "Do you wear glasses?"

Powers: "No. My vision is 20-20."

Me: "What were you doing at the time you saw this person on the stairs?"

Powers: "I work as a musician. I was coming home from a gig."

Me: "What gig?"

Powers: "A gig at a local hotel. The Oceanfront Arms."

Me: "Had you had anything to drink? As in alcohol?"

Powers: "No. I was sober. I don't do drugs either."

Me: "So how good a look did you get at this person on the stairs?"

Powers: "She was in shadow, but I could see enough to tell it was a tall, thin dark woman."

Me: "When you picked her out of the lineup, what made you so sure you picked the right one?"

Powers: "The build, the clothing, her complexion. It was all as I remembered it."

Me: "But you say her face was in shadow?"

Powers: "Well … yes, but …"

Me: "What?"

Powers: "I could still see enough of her features to be sure it was her."

Me: "You're certain?"

Powers: "Absolutely. Was there anything else?"

After attempting to pick apart his version of that night with a few more questions, I called it quits. However, I wondered how much more there was to his story.

CHAPTER TWENTY-ONE

I was going to drive the few blocks back to the condo, but I was too wired from all that damned coffee. I headed toward Coastal Highway instead. Tomorrow was Thursday. Hell, it was already Thursday.

Conference attendees would probably appear in force on Friday. A few early birds might show tomorrow—I meant today. Snap!

In the meantime, had Betsy Larkin heard about Jamila on the news and pulled her from the program? And what about Jinx? Time was running out. I needed answers, right now. And I could barely keep track of what day it was.

I pulled up at the red light at the intersection and considered which way to go. North toward Delaware? South toward downtown? Did it matter? At this time of night, nothing was going on in either place.

Curtis Little was dead. Who would have killed him? Did it have anything to do with Billy Ray's murder? Were they completely unrelated? What were the chances?

Thoughts were careering through my overcaffeinated brain like rabid gerbils. Then another one jumped out: *what the hell has Conroy been doing?* My overheated ponderings wound down like a wheezing diesel engine.

Just what had that patronizing son of a bitch been up to, anyhow?

As if on autopilot, I made a left toward his house after the light turned green. I had no clue what I intended to do when I got there.

The highway had fewer cars, but more than I'd expect at that hour of the morning. Probably underage drinkers. June bugs out on the town. I did my best to play keep-away from the ones weaving from lane to lane.

Ocean City isn't exactly Las Vegas, but it does have all-night miniature golf courses. So, maybe closer to Disney, without the costumed characters. Add in the many T-shirt shops and candy stores and all-you-can-eat buffets and it's almost Vegas, minus the gambling and the leggy showgirls.

When you reach the north end, the high-rise condos are more evocative of Miami, although the resemblance ends there. Just try and find a Cuban anything.

I reached Conroy's street and made the turn. I had no idea what I expected to find. What I didn't expect to find were lights on in his house and two cars parked in front—Conroy's blue Toyota and one I didn't recognize. Now who could be visiting at this hour, apart from a hyperactive attorney with time on her hands and nowhere else to go?

CHAPTER TWENTY-TWO

Okay, I thought. Don't be ridiculous. Conroy might have a female visitor. He's entitled to a social life.

Assuming that's who the visitor was. I hate assumptions.

I noted the car was a silver late-model compact with Delaware tags.

So, now what? Bust in on Conroy at nearly 3:00 in the morning, probably *in flagrante delicto*?

The guy already loved me, so that would go over really well.

I pulled up to the curb across the street and watched the house. In a window, a shadow flickered past the blind. Then another.

"Hmm." I squirmed and tapped a staccato beat on the wheel. Minutes passed. Ten. Fifteen. Nothing.

As my watch crept up on the twenty-minute mark, I prepared to exit the car, figuring I'd sneak up to a window and take a peek inside. That's when I saw it coming up the street. The beat-up green Chevy with the walleyed headlights.

I slammed the door shut, started the car and took off. The green Chevy did a three-point turn in a driveway and followed.

"What the hell?" I muttered. I put my foot to floor and careened out onto the highway, tires screeching.

The green Chevy lumbered around the corner and roared after me.

Despite the hour, I still had to contend with some traffic. Very little, but enough to make driving 80 miles an hour a bit more than a walk in the park. No choice. Whatever it took, I had to get rid of this pest on my tail.

One problem: I was headed straight into downtown Ocean City. I needed to go in the other direction. On this course, I'd end up at a dead end and a turnabout. I kept going, not knowing what else to do, zooming by block after block. I glanced up in the rear view. The Chevy was gaining on me.

But Jamila's Beemer had the power to go toe-to-toe with the vintage muscle car. I stood on the gas pedal. I was almost airborne. Gaining distance now. I passed a bus and cut in front with room to spare. Smashed my foot on the brake. Made a quick turn at the next street. Kept going, checking the rear view. No sign of the Chevy. Must have passed the street. I turned into a deserted alley, jerked to a stop and gulped air.

Once I'd brought my breathing under control, I asked myself who the hell would want to follow me and why.

I thought back to when I'd first seen the green car. My gut clenched.

The car had first appeared at Curtis Little's trailer park, the last time I'd tried to see him. The last time, as far as I knew, that he'd been alive.

φφφ

All right. If I assumed that Little was involved in illicit drug trafficking with Dwayne Sutterman, perhaps the people in the green car had something to do with that. Or not. I was too tired to think straight and way too wired, especially after racing like a stunt driver down Coastal Highway, to just go home and go to bed.

I placed my forehead on the wheel and let my mind go blank for a moment.

It was Thursday and time was ticking down until Jamila's presentation. Plus Jinx was threatening to expose everything about my ill-advised fling with Ray unless I played ball with her. And I felt no closer to understanding anything.

I closed my eyes and drifted off for a moment.

I opened them and jerked upright. The sky was still dark, but lightening to the east. I checked my watch. 5.30? Good grief. I rubbed my eyes. I had a crick in my neck. My forehead felt sore where it had lain against the wheel. I massaged both areas.

Then my phone rang.

I picked it up and opened it.

"Yeah." I sounded like a groaning wooden board.

"Sam?" It was Jamila. She sounded worried.

"Hi. Yeah. Don't worry. I'm fine." I sputtered the words. I couldn't seem to make long sentences.

"Where've you been all night?"

"Uhhhh." This was about the most articulate thing I could conjure up. "We'll talk later, okay?"

I disconnected before she could ask more and turned off the phone.

After taking a moment to get my bearings, I started the car and headed back toward the highway. The dark-blue eastern sky was striped with fiery orange and salmon pink. I succumbed to temptation and turned left into a parking area near the boardwalk.

Pulling into a spot and locking the car, I climbed the ramp to the boardwalk and crossed to the rail. I leaned on the cold metal and felt the refreshing ocean breeze blow against me. The horizon blazed in Technicolor shades of pink, yellow, and blue along with the hot reddish-orange ball of the sun. Above the water, gulls circled and cried mournfully. A lone bicyclist rolled down the boardwalk behind me.

I shivered and crossed my arms. The beach was desolate. The waves washing up on the sand seemed less soothing than corrosive. Pounding the shore, over and over.

I stood alone and watched, a stranger in a strange land. Feeling no more welcome than a visitor from an alien planet.

φφφ

After a good half hour watching the sun come up and feeling sorry for myself, I pulled it together. I wasn't going to accomplish anything standing there staring at the beach.

"C'mon, Sam," I muttered. "You've been in tougher spots than this. Get going."

I turned and marched back to the ramp, descending to the lot where the car was parked. I unlocked the car, slid inside, inserted the key and turned it. Nothing happened.

"What the f-!"

If it had been my car, I wouldn't have been surprised. My old '67 Mustang was a purple piece of shit on wheels. But this was Jamila's Beemer. I tried the key again. Nothing. No click, no grumble of an engine trying to start.

"Ohhh!" I could have wept. I sat, staring straight ahead, and realized the hood looked slightly bent. And not quite closed. Like it had been jimmied open.

"Fuck me!" I jumped out and ran to the front of the car. I could easily see the damage now. I jiggled the catch and opened the hood fully. Wires had been pulled out all over. A random act of vandalism.

"Fucking June bugs," I said to myself. Or was it? Who else could have done this? Who else indeed?

CHAPTER TWENTY-THREE

I was no closer to finding Billy Ray's real killer, and I'd managed to get Jamila's car vandalized. Now, I'd have the thankless job of explaining that to her, made doubly hard by staying out all night then hanging up after she'd called to make sure I was okay.

I held my throbbing head in my hands and squeezed my eyes shut, hoping it was all a terrible nightmare. I ventured to open them and, unfortunately, it was all too real.

Heaving a sigh, I slammed the hood shut, locked the car and started walking.

At barely the crack o' dawn, I chose not to call Jamila right away about the car. I burned with guilt. I hoped that she'd simply gone back to sleep and thought no more about me after I'd ended our call so summarily. Didn't she have enough problems?

The odor of fried eggs, potatoes, and coffee lured me. When was the last time I'd eaten? My stomach felt hollow as a basketball. A gurgling basketball. I followed the scent to a corner café. Like a lemming drawn over a cliff, I lunged through the door and made for the counter.

The waitress, her curly red hair bound up in a net, bounced around the joint in a light blue waitress outfit. She held a coffee pot in one hand and wore a large lipsticked smile. Bright red. Naturally, her name was Flo. She filled a nearby customer's cup, chattering nonstop, and sauntered my way.

"How's it hangin', hon?" she asked, pen poised over pad.

"Great," I said, lying like a rug. "Can I get a waffle, three scrambled eggs, two sides of bacon, a side of potatoes, and all the coffee you can spare me? And throw in a blueberry muffin, while you're at it."

"Hmm. Looks like someone's hungry. Ooh, I'm jealous, girl. How do you stay so thin? Look at you."

"Well … I don't eat like this all the time." *Please, please. Just fill my order. We'll chat later.*

"It's metabolism, you know? You lucky thing." She paused and leaned in. "Anything else?" Her lips compressed into a knowing smirk.

"No. Yes. Well, could I get the muffin and coffee first?" *Please, please, please …*

"Sure, hon." She flounced off and returned with both. It took great restraint not to stuff the whole muffin into my mouth.

Later, as I gobbled my breakfast, Flo entertained with her running commentary. She could have done a solo Broadway show. "The Vagina Diner Monologues." Flo was funny in the way that small-town waitresses can be. And friendly? Other than Amber at FPL, she was the nicest person I'd dealt with lately. While I harbored thoughts of asking her to run for mayor, Flo said something that snapped me from my reverie.

"Hear about that murder at Bower Farms last night?"

"Murder? You're kidding." A man two stools down spoke.

"Well, according to the news I heard on the radio this morning, they think the dead guy might have been smuggling illegal aliens."

The man snorted. "Shit. Spics. The guy got killed smuggling Spics into the country? Spics who take our jobs? Serves him right, I say. Son of a bitch."

I could feel my face grow hot and my temper rise. *Spics, my ass. And whose jobs are they taking? The ones you don't want. The ones that pay shit.*

I did a long, slow count to ten. Then twenty. Forced myself to breath deeply, in and out. I had enough problems without going off on a local redneck.

"Stan, they aren't all bad," Flo replied. "Some of them work damned hard. They do work no one else will take. Construction, landscaping, poultry work, crab meat processing. Thankless stuff that doesn't pay. God knows, I should know about that."

I looked up at Flo with new appreciation. She sauntered over, her coffee-pot appendage at the ready. "More?"

I smiled. "No thanks. I think I've had enough."

I settled my bill with Flo who doubled as cashier, pressing a ten-dollar tip into her hand. She looked at me as if I'd lost my mind.

"You obviously work very hard," I said. "And you just made my morning. Thank you."

With that, I got up and walked away. But not before catching the smile on her face.

φφφ

With a full stomach, I couldn't postpone the inevitable any longer. I had to make the call to Jamila about her car. I turned on my phone, expecting messages from her. None were there.

I expected to reach an angry friend. She wasn't. In fact, she took the news about her car with astonishing poise and grace, saying that she'd get in touch with her insurance company about securing a rental. Her comprehensive insurance would cover all of it, of course. I guess when you're a murder suspect, having your car fucked with is pretty low on your list of concerns.

She even forgave me for hanging up on her after I told her about my lovely evening—summoned by an anonymous call to another murder scene, arriving at Conroy's house to find him in a mysterious meeting with someone or other, fleeing God knows who in an old Chevy during a high-speed chase down Coastal Highway.

"I passed out in the car, and when I woke up, the sun was rising," I explained.

"Don't worry about it. Sounds like you've been through hell."

Well, what about you?

"Are you all right?"

The breathy sound of a sigh. "Yeah, I'm okay."

"Any more media calls?"

"A few."

Shit. I wondered how long we could hold off that pack of jackals. In fact, I wondered if any of them were exploring possible connections between last night's murder at Bower Farms and Billy Ray's unfortunate demise.

"Sam, I should probably call the insurance company." Jamila's voice snapped me back to attention.

"Right. Good idea."

"You'll need a car, won't you?"

I looked up the street and spotted a scooter rental outfit. "Not necessarily."

φφφ

Ocean City is two-wheeled rental central. You can find just about any kind of two-wheeled transportation you might desire for rent within the city limits. Scooters have become an extremely popular mode of transport in this town, given the high price of gas and the low availability of parking. Rather than risk Jamila's wheels, I'd get my own. Why blow bucks on a car, if I could get by with less? The scooter was speedy and cheap. Highly maneuverable in traffic. I took it for a test ride on the straightaway of Coastal Highway. This baby could move. It maxed out at a blinding 45 miles per hour, though it felt like closer to 60. So, I backed her down quickly.

As I played with my new toy, I pondered where to go next. If the police suspected Curtis Little of smuggling illegal workers, I wondered how much evidence they had. I also wondered if Little and Sutterman could have been smuggling people and drugs in a joint operation. How interesting would that be? And what proof did I have? None, of course. What else was new?

Think, Sam. Where to start looking? How about Little's trailer? Haven't the cops been there? Perhaps not. Maybe they haven't gotten a warrant yet. So what are you waiting for?

I pulled the scooter over and called Amber's cell number. She answered on the second ring.

"Hi there," I said. "I need a Spanish translator. How'd you like to do something a bit different this morning?"

CHAPTER TWENTY-FOUR

I'd managed to catch Amber before she left for work. Although she hadn't planned on making a trip to Curtis Little's trailer, I stressed that the cops could be obtaining a warrant as we spoke, making time a factor. I assumed they suspected Little of smuggling illegals based on evidence obtained at his workplace or around the crime scene. Invading his home would require probable cause, which I was pretty sure they were trying to establish with a judge at that very moment. Before they did, I wanted to take a look inside that trailer and see if anything connected Little's death with Billy Ray's. This meant, if I hoped to find anything, I needed to act fast.

I made a quick stop at Jamila's car to transfer a few personal belongings into the scooter's storage compartment before taking off to meet Amber at a mutually convenient parking lot. We took her car to Little's trailer. A knock at the door and Carmen answered.

"Hola, Carmen," I said. "Me llamo, Sam."

"Sí" She smiled and nodded. "Recuerdo."

"Carmen … uh …" I gestured back and forth between the two women. "Amber Moore."

Amber picked up the ball and started rattling off Spanish. Carmen responded in kind. I stood there, grinning. This went on for a bit. Carmen invited us in. Apparently. We went in. I kept grinning and nodding. Carmen took on a slightly alarmed look. Amber's voice assumed a soothing quality. She placed a comforting hand on Carmen's arm. The woman seemed somewhat appeased, but still wary. Amber paused and said, "I asked if the police have been here. She freaked a bit. She claims her work visa is valid, but I wonder, you know?"

"Yeah, I know." I said, sotto voce. A bit louder, I added, "Excuse me, Carmen, dónde está, um, el baño?"

Carmen pointed toward the other end of the double-wide. A bathroom door was on the right, next to a small room with a bed and dresser. A dresser full of drawers. "A la derecha," she said.

"To the right," Amber translated.

"Got it," I said. "Can you, um, keep her occupied?"

"Sam …"

"I need to duck in there for a quick peek before the cops come in and scoop everything up."

Amber sucked in a quick breath. "Okay." She turned toward Carmen and guided her toward a sofa, keeping her facing away from me. Together, they sat and gabbed about whatever. I scurried down the hall, bypassing the bathroom, slipping into the bedroom, and began rifling through the dresser drawers as fast as I possibly could.

I pulled the first one open only to find socks and underwear. The second one revealed shirts and long johns. The third one contained some official-looking paperwork, but I didn't have the time to sort it all out. The whole enterprise began to feel like an exercise in futility until I opened the bottom drawer. It was jammed with rows of Social Security cards and visas marked "H-2A." I searched my memory. Hadn't Amber mentioned something about these visas? I'd stake my next retainer that these allowed foreigners to do seasonal agricultural work in the United States.

This was it. The first real lead I'd found. But to where? What did it signify? The Social Security cards and visas were obvious fakes. So this confirmed that Curtis Little was indeed involved in smuggling illegals into the country. But why was he killed? And what, if anything, did it have to do with Billy Ray's death?

My muddled thoughts were interrupted by pounding on the door.

I heard it open.

"Police," a man said. "We have a warrant to search the premises."

CHAPTER TWENTY-FIVE

While Amber and Carmen distracted the cops, I slunk into the tiny bathroom. I flushed the toilet, ran the tap several seconds, then left and walked toward the visitors, slapping my hands against my jeans.

And who led this contingent? The short craggy-faced cowboy with the calloused hands.

"Good morning," I said. "Detective Morgan, isn't it?"

"Amos Morgan, ma'am." He delivered the line in a near monotone. "Funny you should be here."

I shrugged. "I was in the neighborhood. Carmen and I have met. You can ask her. Right, Carmen?"

I gave Carmen my most disarming grin. She nodded and smiled brightly, clearly not understanding a word.

"I take it you want to search the trailer?" I said. "I don't want to get in your way." I glanced at Amber, who grabbed her purse and joined me. "So unless you have further business with us, we'll be going."

"What are you doing here?" Morgan dug in like a pit bull.

"Paying our respects."

He scowled. "Sure you were."

"Detective, you have no cause to hold us."

Morgan said nothing. Our gazes, as they say, locked. I tore mine loose from his. "Let's go," I said, and ushered Amber out the door. As we hustled to the car, I noticed that one of the official vehicles bore an EPA logo. *What's that about?* We beat feet out of there before you could say the words "Terry stop."

φφφ

"Wow. That was close," Amber said. We rolled down Route 50 toward the lot where I'd parked the scooter.

"You bet." Close in more ways than one. What if Morgan had decided the calls from Little's phone to mine provided the specific and articulable facts needed to do a Terry stop? That is, what if he'd decided they gave him cause to hold me under *Terry v. Ohio*, the case every law student and criminal lawyer knows inside and out? A Terry stop is supposed to apply to stop-and-search cases for weaponry. But what comfort was that? These days, cops will try to bend the Fourth Amendment every which way. And case law can be modified. But I'd managed to get out of harm's way. For the moment.

"Now," I said, parroting Mulrooney. "Did you notice one of the cars back there had an EPA logo? Clearly, they're not interested in illegal immigrants. So, any idea why EPA would be involved?"

Amber's eyebrows did a brief mating dance. "Well, one of the things EPA has been doing is trying to get bigger companies like Perdue to make sure the farmers they work with maintain high environmental compliance standards."

"Okay. So how does this work?"

"Years ago, Perdue signed a memorandum of understanding with EPA. It created the Perdue Clean Waters Environmental Initiative. The idea is that Perdue will help provide technical assistance and training, as well as monitoring and compliance, to make sure their poultry providers are doing business in an environmentally sound way."

I nodded. "But this doesn't bind Bower Farms legally, does it?"

Amber shook her head. "No, but it does provide a template for other socially conscious companies. And many companies have become interested in following Perdue's example. It gives them a much better image, particularly among investors who care about environmental effects and corporate accountability. Not to mention creating goodwill with environmentalist groups and the public."

Hmm, I thought. I wondered how many smaller companies just pretend to be socially conscious and get away with it. All that paperwork stuck in the drawer. If only I'd had a chance to look it over.

"Oh, by the way," Amber said, interrupting my thoughts. "Carmen mentioned that Curtis often talked to a woman named Maria on the phone."

"Maria Benitez?

"She didn't know her last name."

Great. Maria was only among the most popular female Hispanic names out there. And Maria Benitez was almost as common as Mary Jones.

"The only other lead I have is the name Maria Benitez. Any chance she might be a worker or related to someone who works for Bower?"

Amber shrugged. "It's a common name, but I know someone who might know."

She pulled the car over to the shoulder and dug her cell phone out of her shoulder bag. "Let me make a call and see if my source is okay with talking to you."

φφφ

Two minutes of fast-talking Spanish later, we were back on the road. "It's fine," Amber said. "As long as you're not with immigration or the cops, they'll answer questions."

Ten minutes after that, we pulled up before a tiny house that would have accommodated Little's double-wide, if you knocked down the inner walls. The dying lawn stretched roughly twenty feet from the house and clung to the curb. Toys were strewn about here and there. Off to the side, a rusty bicycle leaned against a trash can.

Amber put the car in park, gathered her things, and exited the vehicle. I got out and eyed the place. Where were the kids? The place looked deserted. How much worse could it be than the ghettos of Bed-Stuy, where I grew up? Or the ones where I'd spent time searching for evidence in a haunting case I'd handled only last fall.

We negotiated the buckled concrete walkway to the front door. Amber knocked three times. Birds sang cheerful morning songs. Strange muzak. After a lengthy wait, the door creaked open. A short, brown man around forty or so, wearing faded jeans and a white wife-beater shirt, stood in the doorway. He leaned on a set of crutches, his right foot encased in plaster.

"Can you tell him who I am?" I asked Amber.

Amber leaned toward me. "I know. I'll make the introductions, tell him who you represent, then ask him if he's ever heard of Maria Benitez. Okay?"

That seemed simple enough, so I nodded.

Amber turned toward the man and engaged him in conversation in Spanish. He nodded. I heard her mention Maria's name. He nodded some more. Interesting. But then he shook his head.

"Gracias," Amber said. She turned to me. "He says that one of the women living here has mentioned the name Maria Benitez on occasion. However, he doesn't know anything else about her."

"Okay. Could you ask him, who lives here and where are they? Who is the woman who mentioned Maria and where is she?"

Amber relayed my questions to him in Spanish. He responded.

"They're all working right now," she said. "Luisa works as a crab picker. You'll find her at the processing plant about half a mile from here."

"Is Luisa his wife?"

"No, she's his cousin." Amber turned to face me directly. "He says five families live here. That's pretty typical. And I've seen much worse."

φφφ

When Amber and I reached the processing plant, she said, "Why don't I go in and see if I can find Luisa and sneak her out here? She may feel uncomfortable being asked questions in the presence of her coworkers."

"Sure," I said.

She left the car and entered the building.

I sat alone, glancing from side to side. Just how big was this operation we were unearthing, anyway?

Was the CIA going to swoop in at any moment?

I laughed. "Good God, Sam. Don't be ridiculous." I said out loud.

Then, I heard the gunshot and flung myself down on the front seat.

CHAPTER TWENTY-SIX

I pulled myself upright in the seat, feeling like an idiot.

I'd been so wrapped up in my thoughts, I hadn't noticed the truck pull up to the loading dock only about fifty feet away. And when the damn thing backfired, I could've sworn it was a gunshot.

I had just collected my wits, when Amber emerged from the building with a stocky brown woman in tow. The woman's hair was pulled back and tucked under a ball cap. She wore a striped T-shirt, jeans, and a worried look.

Amber hustled Luisa into the car's back seat, murmuring in Spanish. Luisa looked from Amber to me, brown eyes growing wider by the second.

"I've explained who you are and that you need to know about Maria Benitez. Do you have more specific questions?" Amber asked.

"Luisa, what have you heard about Maria and Bower Farms?"

Amber translated. Luisa shook her head. "Nada," she said. Amber shrugged.

"What about Maria and Dwayne Sutterman?"

Amber started to translate, but Luisa said, "Doo-ah-ee-nay? He no good."

"Why do you say that?" I persisted. "¿Porqué?"

Amber rattled off the translation. Luisa responded.

Amber said, "She says that Dwayne is a drug dealer who uses her people to buy or distribute for him. She thinks Maria Benitez is his supplier."

φφφ

In the ten minutes I got with Luisa, I gleaned more information from her. Apart from the fact that Dwayne Sutterman was more than the occasional user, that is. For starters, she was lucky to be living in a one-bedroom dump with four other families instead of a company-owned trailer with a nonworking sewage system and other delightful perks that she couldn't complain about for fear of incurring her employer's wrath and the government's scrutiny of her legal status. Further, her kids were, in fact, working by her side today. Well, the family that picks together sticks together, right?

Finally, Luisa suggested I try looking for more information about Dwayne at the trailer park where she used to live. A place where the most desperate people would seek extra income through extralegal means.

φφφ

The trailers jammed into Luisa's former neighborhood made Curtis Little's double-wide look like the Waldorf Astoria. A dirt road encircled the trailer park. We took it around, surveying the place, until we returned to the entrance. The place was practically buried in dust and reeked of raw sewage. A couple of swarthy men dressed in jeans and T-shirts sat in lawn chairs next to a trailer, tipping back beers. I checked my watch. 8:15? A little early for poultry workers or crab pickers. But not drug dealers.

"Amber, I want to question those guys," I said, pointing to the men.

Amber looked unsure, but nodded. She pulled the car over and cut the ignition.

We got out and walked toward the men, who were laughing and carrying on a raucous Spanish conversation. They paid no heed to us, but kept it up, even as I appeared right beside them.

"Hola," I said.

One of them snickered. The other one sneered and took another swig of beer.

"Do you know Dwayne Sutterman?" I asked.

Mr. Snickers froze. Clearly, someone understood English. The Beer Swigger swallowed with an audible gulp and belched.

I reached for my wallet and pulled out a fifty-dollar bill. "What can I get for this?"

The Beer Swigger laughed. "I sell you all the beer in my fridge. How 'bout that?"

After ten minutes of fruitless questioning, it became clear that these guys were probably drug dealers, and they weren't going to help me in any way, shape, or form. So Amber and I got back in the car and split.

"There's got to be something I can follow up on," I said. "I'm running out of time."

I thought again about the EPA's interest. Was there anything there to explore?

"You know, I'd really be interested in pursuing this environmental compliance angle a bit further," I said. "Would you happen to know if Bower Farms used a consultant on these issues?"

Amber said, "I might have a possible contact you could try."

Amber dropped me off at my scooter and I followed her to the office in Salisbury. There she rummaged through her files, looking for a letter or note or some scrap of information that might help.

"This isn't something we keep regular records on," she said. "Sorry."

"Don't worry about it," I assured her, checking my watch. Almost 8:45.

She turned her attention to the papers strewn across her desk, pawing through them. "I could have sworn I had … yes!" She snatched up a business card and presented it to me with a flourish. "There you go. I got her card at a recent conference. I'm pretty sure she said they've specialized in start-ups, like Bower Farms."

I took a look at the card. It read: *Greener Way Consultants.* The slogan read, "Do green business and make more green."

I peered closer at the name and title in smaller print under the company name: *Karla Dixon, CEO and Founder.*

Well, if it wasn't Big Red. What do you know?

CHAPTER TWENTY-SEVEN

It was just past 10:30 when I marched up the steps of the blue and gray building in West Ocean City, strode the walkway to Unit #204 and rapped on the door.

No answer. I rang the bell and waited. Nothing.

I pounded on the door. Hard.

I could sense her presence on the other side. Waiting.

I rang the bell again. Over and over. And over.

"Go away!" A muffled voice sounded from inside.

"Avon calling!" I said.

"I'll call the cops."

"Oh, good. We can both talk to them about Greener Way Consultants and Billy Ray. Won't that be fun?"

Silence. The door opened a crack, which widened to reveal Karla. She was dressed in a purple tank top, frayed cutoffs and flip flops.

Well, this is interesting, but I don't have all day.

"Karla, you forged documents, didn't you—?"

"Wait, wait! Come in. Come in."

Suddenly, Karla had become my best buddy. She couldn't drag me into her condo fast enough. She certainly wasn't slamming the door in my face this time.

"Can I get you a drink? Coffee? Water?" Karla hovered near me.

"No, thanks. This won't take long."

I settled onto the sofa and Karla perched on the other end, hands twisting in her lap.

"Karla, what if I told you the EPA is helping to investigate Curtis Little's murder? And they're searching his trailer right about now? And what if I told you I found false compliance documents for poultry producers that Bower Farms did business with? And that those documents were prepared by your company—Greener Way Consultants—and had your signature on them?

"And what if I also told you I found them in Curtis Little's trailer? Would that suggest a possible motive for his murder do you think?"

Karla's face turned chalk white. "No! I didn't. I swear. It wasn't me."

"Did Curtis try to blackmail you?"

Tears leaked from Karla's eyes. She nodded.

I moved down the sofa and sat next to Karla, placing a reassuring hand on her shoulder. "Tell me what happened."

Karla sobbed and hiccupped. Finally, she said, "Curtis was greedy. He felt he wasn't getting his fair share."

"Fair share of what?"

"We all took a cut of the larger operation."

"Which was?"

"I didn't ask questions."

Yeah, I thought. I'll bet.

"We were supposed to get equal shares," she continued. "But Curtis said he wanted more, since he brought the workers in. That's all I know. Honest!"

"So, what were you paid for?"

"Billy Ray knew the company couldn't afford the kind of oversight program that the big companies like Perdue have. So he came to me and asked a favor. I did all the paperwork and he got his good PR in return. After that, he treated me like a goddamn queen. He couldn't afford not to, right?"

What was I hearing? Regret? Bitterness? Rage? Self-hatred?

I couldn't help myself. I had to ask.

"Karla, did you love Billy Ray? Or did you do it just for the money?"

She snorted. "What do you think?"

I shook my head. "Like I'd know?"

"Well, now what?" Karla said, backhanding the tears from her cheeks.

"Tell me the truth. Is Dwayne Sutterman's illegal drug trafficking part of the larger operation?"

Karla shook her head. "I don't know, but I wouldn't doubt it." She stared at her lap.

Not an admission, but not a denial, either. "Do you know where he works?"

Karla laughed bitterly. "Dwayne works with the watermen, to the extent he works at all. When he's not hanging out at his place, huffing weed, he's either in a boat on the water or drinking beer with the other lowlifes at the Pirate's Den down near the inlet."

"I see." I rose. "Have you ever heard of Maria Benitez?"

This drew a perplexed look and shake of her head.

"Okay," I said. "I have to go now. Thanks for confirming my theory."

"What?"

I leaned toward her. "Karla, here's a tip. When a lawyer says something in the form of a question, it's usually a hypothetical. Now do you understand?"

CHAPTER TWENTY-EIGHT

The Pirate's Den was a ramshackle building with weathered driftwood boards stacked into makeshift walls. I parked the scooter in the lot and climbed the wooden ramp to the entrance. A pirate's skull-and-crossbones sign welcomed me. Cute.

I pulled open the door and stared into a void. The bar was so dimly lit, I had to step inside and let my eyes adjust before I could see a thing. It took a while. Eventually I made out a bar running along the back wall, old-fashioned lanterns hung on wrought iron posts, wooden beams, starfish, shells and other beachy doodads hanging from the fishnet on the walls. A few customers emerged from the dark.

Now what? Should I shout, "Ahoy?" Blow a foghorn?

I chose to move toward the bar, where a tall steroid addict was wiping the counter.

"Excuse me, sir," I said, drawing him aside to speak out of earshot of the local drunks. "I wonder if you could help me."

Goliath glanced my way. "What'll it be, lady?"

"I'll have a ginger ale. Has Dwayne Sutterman been in today?"

He stopped wiping. He turned and gazed down at me. "Who wants to know?"

I pulled the fifty-dollar bill from my wallet and waved it in his face. "Does it really matter?"

My eyes had fully adjusted to the gloom, so I could see him squinting, brow creased in apparent thought.

"So, can I have my ginger ale, please?" I asked.

"Lady, ginger ale only costs a couple of bucks."

"I know. But I tip well." I folded the note and tapped it on the bar. "If the service is good enough."

He tossed the rag aside, rattled some ice into a glass and hosed my drink into being. He produced a small napkin and placed it on the bar before setting the glass on it. He even gave me a straw.

"How's that?" he asked.

"Nice," I said. "But not worth fifty bucks."

He exhaled. He actually seemed to shrink a bit.

"Okay," he said. "You didn't hear this from me." He leaned closer. "Dwayne was in here earlier. Word is he's going down to the docks today. From the looks of it, he might be taking a long trip."

"Uh huh. And which dock?"

He gave me the name of a marina and a dock number. A place less than half a mile from the Pirate's Den.

"Thanks, man." I gave him the fifty. "Who says there's no such thing as good service, anymore?"

φφφ

By the time I reached the marina, it was almost 11:30. Most of the watermen were out, so it wasn't hard to spot Dwayne's boat, *The Wet Dream.*

If the boat was Dwayne's idea of a wet dream, I had to wonder. Given its small size and relative state of disrepair, I thought *The Rusty Bucket* would have been more appropriate.

I strolled down the pier toward *The Wet Dream.* Dwayne must have disappeared down the hatch or whatever it's called. I stood watch over the floating piece of shit. Surely, he wasn't expecting to get far in this thing, was he?

I don't know a damn thing about boats, but *The Wet Dream* was skuzzy, with slime growing like moss along the sides. Were those tiny shells clinging to the hull barnacles or what?

Dwayne popped out of the hatch, like a stripper from a cake. Surprise!

I took a moment to recover. "Hi, Dwayne."

He scowled. He was good at that. "How the hell did you get here?"

"On my scooter." Well, he asked.

"I mean, how did you know I was here?"

"I was told."

"Who told you?"

"Does it matter?"

"Yes."

"Can we skip the repartee? I'm not telling you." Dwayne continued to scowl. A world champion scowler, that guy.

"Where are you going?" I asked.

"Out to sea," he said. "Fishing. Crabbing. Whatever."

"Really? You're leaving a bit late, aren't you? Most fishermen go out early. I bet they're out there, reeling in their catches as we speak."

"I can leave whenever I want," Dwayne said. "I don't have to punch a clock. I don't have to account for my time."

"I don't know much about crabbing, but I don't see any equipment on this rattrap that even remotely resembles what you'd need to do any serious crabbing."

Dwayne crossed his arms. "What do you want?" he asked. His jaw worked hard enough to make my head hurt.

"What was your part in killing Curtis Little?"

Dwayne tossed his head back and laughed.

"Who killed Billy Ray?" I asked.

Dwayne shook with laughter. Apparently, I'd missed my calling as a stand-up comic.

"I know you're part of a larger scheme. Something involving drugs. When they arrest Karla Dixon, she may not know the details, but I'm sure she'll lead the cops to you. Do you really think you're going to escape in that dinky little boat?"

Dwayne stopped laughing, but he grinned at me and wiped his eyes.

"You have no idea," he said. "You don't know who you're dealing with. You're in way over your head."

"Who is Maria Benitez?"

His grin vanished. He went below and slammed the hatch.

CHAPTER TWENTY-NINE

Now I knew four things. Curtis Little had definitely been involved in smuggling illegal workers into the country, Karla Dixon was more than just a busty redhead, Dwayne Sutterman was way more than a pothead and occasional fisherman, and there was something distinctly rotten going on at Bower Farms. No wonder those three had latched onto Billy Ray.

So why would they want to kill the goose that provided their golden eggs? I could understand how Curtis Little might have gotten killed due to greed, but why Billy Ray? What motive would his minions have?

As I motored down the road, I grasped at straws. What should I do next? My mind meandered through the past few days. I thought about my talk with Danni Beranski. Had I asked her about Bower's son, Junior? What had she said? That he wasn't cut out to take over the business? Could it be he'd felt deprived of his birthright?

Maybe I needed to meet the guy.

After all, this was a small community. And word got around. What if Marshall Jr. heard about the confrontation? What if he wanted to take over the business in Billy Ray's stead? And what if he knew about this "big operation," whatever it comprised? Could this all add up to a couple of murders? One of which he'd conveniently pinned on Jamila, based on circumstance?

My mind was reeling. But it was a theory. Hell, it was a start. And it would explain why Marshall Bower, Sr., if he knew or suspected that his son killed his stepson and wanted to protect Junior, wouldn't talk to me without a lawyer present. Speculation? Yes. Next step? Find proof.

I pulled onto the shoulder, dug my notebook out of my shoulder bag and checked the address I'd jotted down for Marshall Bower's home. It was time to pay the Bower family a visit. I tucked the notebook away and hit the road.

φφφ

Twenty minutes later I motored up to an 8-foot-high wrought-iron gate. The kind with spikes on top for the severed heads. A small slate-gray box with blue and yellow buttons and a pinhole-dotted speaker was attached to one side of the entrance. Under the blue button it said, "Press Upon Arrival." The yellow button was labeled "Press to Talk." I pressed the blue button and waited.

A camera perched atop one of the brick columns flanking the gate. No attempt had been made to hide or camouflage it. *Hi there! Welcome to the House of Bower Reality TV Show.* I waved at it. Considered flipping the bird and thought better of it.

The speaker issued a crackled "Yes?"

I hit the talk button. "Hi. Is Junior there?" I was gambling. Couldn't recall if he went by Junior or not. Seemed like he would. Silence ensued. *Shit.*

I wondered if I'd fucked up big time. The speaker squawked. Amid background noise, I heard, "Sorry about the wait. We're around back. C'mon in."

The gate clicked and opened. I eased the scooter through as if two-wheeling into a millionaire's estate was something I did routinely.

I motored up a long, circuitous driveway lined with common-variety trees. The occasional dogwood or magnolia broke the monotony. The air was honey scented. I caught glimpses of white blossoms spiking upward among the greenery. This trip through the Garden of Eden took me to the front entrance of the Bower mansion.

Viewing Chez Bower from the seat of a scooter had a humbling effect.

I gawked at the huge house looming over me—five stories of gabled faux Tudor excess extended left and right for a few thousand miles. The trees along the driveway had given way to a view of a sweeping front yard to rival the gardens of Versailles. Somewhere, I could hear music. Hip-hop? From behind a Tudor home? In Versailles?

As I tried to establish that I was still in touch with reality, a young woman dashed out from the left side of the house, laughing. She raced across the front lawn. Stumbling but managing to stay upright, she ducked beside a tall shrub near the walkway to the front door.

A young man appeared where she'd emerged and looked around. He wore blue swimming trunks.

The young woman noticed me. She put her finger to her lips.

I looked back and arched an eyebrow, but said nothing. The young woman wore absolutely nothing.

CHAPTER THIRTY

The young man in the blue trunks gave me a curious glance then ventured forth as if I weren't there. "Denise!" he called.

I glanced sideways at the woman I assumed was Denise. She crouched behind the bush, snickering into her hand.

"Hi," I said. "Looking for someone?"

The man stopped and gaped at me. Denise stopped snickering and gaped at me. Apparently, people were anxious to show me their dental work.

"Did you see a girl come by here?" the man asked. He crossed the lawn and stood next to me.

"No, I haven't actually." I shot Denise a look. She took her cue and bolted. The young man turned and watched her scamper off, her laughter trailing behind her. Her naked derriere waved a merry farewell to us both.

"Okay, I lied," I said. "Sorry."

The young man shook his head. "Forget it. She's just playing her usual games. She'll come around after she's had a few ..." He did this thing with his thumb and pinkie. Holding them up to his mouth, he tipped them like a drinking glass. Didn't look a bit like a drinking glass, but I got the idea.

"I'm looking for Marshall Bower, Jr.," I said.

The young man grinned. He had sky-blue eyes, tan skin and Robert Redford blond hair. "After you lied to me, you're asking for my help?"

"Now you're just teasing." *Shameless flirt. Jesus. My breakfast would come up if things continued in this vein.*

"Well." The blue eyes glimmered. "I could arrange an introduction."

"Really?" I feigned excitement.

He stuck out his hand. "Hi. I'm Marshall Bower, Jr. Who are you and where have you been all my life?"

I paused a moment, then said, "Sam. My name is Sam McRae."

The pause was to contemplate the pickup line, which was as corny as Kansas in August, as well as the bulge in Junior's swimming trunks.

I left my scooter near the garage. Junior escorted me to the party, in full swing. Young adults in various stages of undress ran around the rear of the house near the pool and tennis court. Music thumped nonstop from oversized speakers.

I leaned toward Junior and yelled into his ear, "I was hoping to talk to you about your dad's business, if I could."

"Business?" He looked at me with a mixture of alarm and cluelessness that signified stupidity. Then, he snapped back into savoir-faire mode. "Hey, sweetheart. Lighten up. This is a party. Have fun." He grabbed my chin with one hand and squeezed it like a favorite uncle. Yuck.

I wandered through the crowd, taking in all the sights. Boy, these people knew how to party considering it was barely afternoon.

A hog turned on a spit over an open fire pit. The crowd pressed in on me. Drinks were being served from a fake tiki hut by white-jacketed black men. A brunette in a bikini drank a radioactive orange concoction and swayed dangerously close to a koi pond. Silicon melons poured from her top. One woman lit up a joint and offered it to me. Mighty tempting, but I declined. My grip on reality was tenuous enough as it was. I didn't need drugs to loosen my hold.

In all the hubbub, I lost Junior and had to hunt for him. I found him with a group hunched over a rattan table snorting a line of what looked like cocaine. I didn't know people did cocaine anymore.

Although I stood about twenty or thirty feet away, Junior spotted me. "Hey, there you are!" He jumped up and bounced to my side in two leaps.

"About your dad's business," I started.

Suddenly, his arms wrapped around me

"Now I've got you," he shouted.

"I don't think so," I yelled back.

He pressed his erection against my leg. "Don't you want some of this, baby?"

"Not really, no."

"Oh, c'mon." His voice became whiny. "Don't be a tease, mama."

He thrust himself repeatedly against me.

"I said *no*."

"You don't mean it."

"Yes, I do."

He kept thrusting.

"Don't. I'm warning you."

"C'mon, mama. Give it up."

He held me with both hands and was humping my leg now. The party continued around us. No one seemed to care. Or notice.

"For the last time. Stop doing that."

"Please, baby. Please …"

I reared my leg back and kneed him in the groin. He shuddered and sank to the ground. Tears sprang to his eyes.

The music continued to thump. People ran around heedless.

I squatted beside him and knelt down to holler into his ear. "I'm not your baby or your mama. And you should've stopped the first time I said no."

He lay curled in a fetal position and gazed at me with hurt puppy-dog eyes, trying to catch his breath. The music pounded mercilessly. Guests rushed past the fallen form, as if he were a broken and forgotten toy.

Above the din, I heard a sharp clapping behind me. Against the rhythm of the music. I turned to see a woman applauding. Tall, blonde, a looker, boobs out to here.

I stood and raised my voice to address her. "I take it you approve?"

"I want to thank you. You saved me the trouble."

"Oh. And you are?"

"Lisa Fennimore. Junior's fiancé."

CHAPTER THIRTY-ONE

For a moment, words failed. I stuck my hand out. "Sam McRae. It's nice to meet you." *Your fiancé is an idiot.*

Lisa smiled, but without mirth. "I know what you're thinking. You must think I'm some kind of sap to put up with Junior's shit."

"That wasn't what I was thinking." *Not in those exact words.*

Lisa drew in a long breath as if poised to dive underwater. She closed her eyes and blew the breath out through pursed lips. She looked at Junior, on the ground still clutching his crotch, and shook her head.

"C'mon," she said. "There's someone who'd like to meet you."

Lisa led me past a small rose garden through a side door into a kitchen larger than my entire apartment. We walked into another room and I realized that the kitchen had two parts. A room where things were cooked and one where the cooked things were consumed: like a breakfast nook, only really big. A nook should be small, right? Whoever heard of a huge nook?

From there, she led me through the dining room with its mahogany table long enough for roughly a thousand people. The walls must have been mighty thick and the windows well insulated, because the noise from the orgy had been reduced to a low rhythmic murmur. Chandeliers dripped with crystals, throwing off flashes of color in the milky light seeping in between the maroon velvet drapes. Lisa stopped and drew them shut with a snap, plunging the room in shadow. Much better.

We marched on in silence. Lisa proceeded toward the stairs and began to climb. I followed her up the zig-zag staircase. When we reached the top, Lisa turned right and headed down the hall. The door at the end was shut. She knocked on it.

"Yes?" A muffled voice came from within.

Lisa opened the door and entered, ushering me in with her.

My first impression was that of a library or den. The walls were almost completely lined with books. My idea of heaven. The floor was covered with a Persian carpet of salmon pink, gray, and turquoise. A dark brown leather chair sat in one corner, a tall lamp behind it.

"Ms. McRae, this is Marshall Bower, Sr."

Lisa's words snapped me to attention. I focused on the man sitting at the desk before me. Late fifties or early sixties. Broad shoulders. Thickening a bit in the middle, perhaps? Graying, but still handsome. The suggestion of Redford looks buried under middle age and too much drink and responsibility. On the desk, a neat stack of papers sat to one side, anchored by a pair of reading glasses. Must have caught him working at home. Bower scrutinized me. Not looking friendly, but not unfriendly either.

"How do you do, sir," I said, attempting a quick recovery. This was a lot to absorb in one morning.

I walked up to the desk and extended a hand. He rose and shook it, giving it a good squeeze. I gave as good as I got. I think it surprised him.

"To what do I owe the pleasure of this visit?" he asked, nodding an invitation to sit. I took him up on it. Lisa took the other vacant chair.

On one of the bookshelves, I saw a framed family photo. A casual group shot with everyone all smiles. Bower, Sr., in younger days with a dark-haired, brown-eyed woman. A beauty. Two children. A girl around eight or nine who resembled her mother and a tow-headed toddler who must have been Junior.

"Sir, as you probably know, I'm assisting—"

"Ms. McRae," Bower waved his hands. "I know who you represent. You came by my office at one point."

Right. You wouldn't see me without a lawyer. Guess you changed your mind.

"I'll admit I was reluctant to talk to you at first," he continued. "However, now that I've thought it over, I see no harm in doing so. I'm just not sure how I can help you."

Yeah, I'll bet you wouldn't mind knowing what I'm trying to find out, huh? And I have no idea how you can help me, either.

"I just wanted to ask you a few questions," I said.

"Okay. Fire away."

I was trying to think of the nicest possible way to put this. But there wasn't one.

"Sir, may I ask, why did you decide to let your stepson run your business instead of your son?"

Lisa barked a laugh. "Oh, Jesus! You're kidding, right?"

Bower held up a hand. "Now, Lisa. Let's be fair."

Lisa could barely contain herself.

"Ms. McRae. You may have noticed that my son isn't exactly the most responsible person," Bower said. "I love him dearly and want to see him do well, but he is not capable of handling great responsibility."

Lisa's expression was contorting as Bower spoke.

"It is my sincere hope that with their impending marriage," Bower continued, "Lisa will have a steadying influence on Junior. That their love and partnership through life will have a salutary effect on him and make him stronger and more capable as a man."

At this point, Lisa lost it. She snickered loudly, then collapsed into guffaws, nearly falling out of the chair.

Bower glared at her.

Pulling herself upright, Lisa faced me.

"Enough of the bullshit. Junior knocked me up. Now he's marrying me. He'll work for my father's business. And we'll babysit him."

CHAPTER THIRTY-TWO

Junior chose this moment to wander in and cross the room. Still in his blue trunks, sans erection.

"Hi, honey," he mumbled, sinking into the reading chair.

"Hi, stupid."

How delightful.

"I don't get it," I said.

"How do you mean?" Lisa asked.

"It's not like you're showing. You could get an abortion. Or give the child up for adoption. Or are you keeping the child as a matter of principle?"

Lisa smiled. The expression didn't reach her eyes. In fact, it seemed to take effort. She crossed her legs and folded her hands in her lap.

"What we have here is a business arrangement," she said.

"Oh, really?" Bower, Sr., smirked. "Was it business you were conducting when you seduced him?"

"Seduced him? Have you seen that guy go to work? Jesus, Daddy-O, he makes the average rabbit look like a fucking monk."

"How dare you use profanity—"

"Oh, can it! I'll use whatever words I want." Lisa was in high dudgeon. "Remember, my father has agreed to take him off your hands. He's giving him a job in his firm."

Bower, Sr., looked at me. "Fennimore Real Estate is one of the biggest realtors and developers on the Eastern Shore. You could say we have mutually agreeable interests. See, Junior didn't exactly graduate magna cum anything."

"He flunked out," Lisa explained.

Bower grimaced. "Anyway. This opportunity arose for Lisa's father to do me the favor of providing Junior with a job. And Lisa's father is a bit old-fashioned."

"He doesn't believe in abortion," I ventured.

Lisa pouted. "He doesn't believe in giving his daughter free access to money without a husband. In order to tap into my trust fund, I have to marry. Since I succumbed to Junior's charms in a moment of weakness." She actually blushed, then recovered. "Anyhow, looks like I have more than one reason to marry now."

My mind reeled. *Yeah, and probably more than one trust fund to bleed.*

"Sooo … " I said. "When's the wedding?"

"In a couple of weeks. A small private ceremony." Lisa smiled, demurely. "Can't wait. Right, hon?"

She'd directed her words to the reading chair, but no response was forthcoming.

"I've told Lisa and Junior I'll cover their honeymoon to Tuscany or the Riviera or Acapulco," Bower, Sr., stated. "A cruise. Whatever they want. When they get back, Junior will start his new job as a real estate agent with Fennimore Realty. A job where he can learn to handle responsibility."

"And make a pile of dough," Lisa added.

Bower Sr., shot me a pained smile. "Junior needs discipline. He needs structure. He needs a guiding hand, a mentor. Fennimore will serve him well in that role. He'll teach him the real estate business, inside and out."

Lisa coughed. "My father and I will provide babysitting services." She snickered again.

Bower's face darkened. He looked sidewise at Lisa, but he didn't argue. "I know I'll be able to count on Lisa to keep Junior straight."

"Oh, I will," Lisa chimed in. "I'll make sure he wears a suit and tie, drag him to all the right parties and keep him from getting arrested."

She turned in her seat and narrowed her eyes at the man in the blue swim trunks shrinking into the corner chair.

"Um, this has been very interesting," I said, struggling to control my gag reflex. "But I still have a few more questions."

Bower folded his hands on the desk and leaned forward, looking expectant. Lisa looked wary. Junior could have been a potted plant.

"Now that Billy Ray is dead, who's next in line to take charge of the poultry business?"

Bower's face took on a ponderous look. He stared at the bookcase behind me. Searching for a title? This stretched on for half a day or so.

"Mr. Bower?" I prompted. "Are you refusing to answer?"

"No. Just thinking about it."

All right. It was personal information, after all. He had no obligation to tell me.

Finally, he unfolded his hands, lifted one and slapped it on the desk blotter. Lisa and I jumped. I think Junior may have twitched a little.

"Forgive my reluctance to tell you personal financial details," Bower said. "But I tend to be very close-mouthed about such things. However, since I have nothing to hide and you are trying to find my stepson's killer, I want to help you. So, unless I change my will, my daughter Marsha will inherit the business."

CHAPTER THIRTY-THREE

"So, your wife won't take over?" I asked.

"My wife will benefit from a trust fund I've established that will protect my assets from estate taxes. I'm sure, as an attorney, you're familiar with such things."

I was, indeed, familiar with such things. I just didn't do that kind of work. I found it intensely boring, for one thing. For another, I had no clients with the kind of moolah Bower had in abundance.

"Yes, I am," I said. I kept my response short, the way they teach you in law school.

"My wife is anything but a business woman. My daughter, on the other hand—"

He stopped short as the door swung open. A brassy blonde pushing her mid forties sashayed in. Her tight purple Capri pants hugged ample hips; a red, purple, and yellow Hawaiian shirt completed the ensemble. With every step, a festive orange drink in her hand sloshed over the rim of its glass, leaving a dark trail on the Persian carpet. Circling the desk, she draped herself over Bower's shoulders.

"Whatcha doing in here, baby?" She slurred. "We gotta party going on."

"Ms. McRae," Bower said. "This is my wife, Georgia Lee."

I rose and extended my hand. "How do you do?"

"Oh, sweetie, I'm doing great. Can'tcha tell?" She managed to push herself upright, wiped a hand on her shirt and thrust it my way. We shook hands. Hers was sticky.

I resumed my seat, wiping my hand discreetly on the seat back as I did so.

"Okay, so your daughter—"

Bower cut me off with a raised hand—and eyebrows. He turned to his wife, putting a hand on each of her cheeks.

"Honey, we're talking business, okay? I'll be down in just a bit."

Then he made smootchie noises, like you would to a baby. My gag reflex flared up again.

Georgia Lee looked like she'd just lost her best friend. "Okay, Daddy. But, hurry up. I'm lonely. And you know how I get when I'm lonely."

In a multicolored blur, she left. No one spoke. Silence pressed in on my ears.

Bower looked paralyzed, then let out a breath. "Yeah."

"So, your daughter would own the business?" I said.

"Yes, yes. Can we make this quick?" Bower was fidgeting, lines creasing his brow. Due to Georgia Lee's randiness? Was that how they met?

"I understand Marsha's gone. Do you still intend to leave her the business?"

"Frankly, I'm … at a loss. She's my only other heir. I want to keep the business in the family. Junior, well … you've seen for yourself. Marsha's got the smarts. I tried to be a mentor to her. I tried to help her get into the right university. I tried to get her onto the right career path. But ever since her mother died, she wouldn't listen to me. She's hated me ever since."

"Do you have any idea where she is?"

Bower shook his head, eyes glistening.

"Marsha's an idiot," Lisa said. "She could have it all." She waved a hand around the room. "But she took her trust fund money and split."

"You wouldn't know where she is, would you?"

"No, and I couldn't care less."

I nodded and stood. I handed each of them a card, including Junior.

I leaned over the slumped figure in the chair, tossed him the card and murmured, "How about it, Junior. Any idea where your sister went?"

For a moment, his eyes flickered with an unidentifiable emotion. But he said nothing.

I rose, turned, and addressed the room. "I think I've heard enough for now."

φφφ

I left the three of them, closing the door and fleeing down the hall. You'd have thought I was being pursued by monsters or evil spirits. In a sense, I believed this to be true. I hit the zig-zag stairway, bounding downward two steps at a time. Evil pervaded these people, I could feel it emanating from Lisa's cold smile. From her calculating eyes. I could feel it in Bower's lack of empathy for his own son. In his lack of willingness to listen to what his own daughter wanted. In his need to shape everyone and everything into what he wanted them to be.

Junior, meanwhile … Jesus! Talk about a pawn. Sure, he was a nitwit. Even so, the price he'd paid for twenty minutes of pleasure—oh, let's get real, probably five, if he was lucky—was his life. As I made my way to the door, my disgust grew. Bile rose in my throat. Years of working with the Public Defender's Office had never made me feel this wretched. At least, the criminals there didn't hide behind phony respectability.

Before I left, I spotted an umbrella stand beside the door. I took a moment to clear my throat of the bilious phlegm, gathered it in my mouth and hocked a loogie into the stand before I walked out.

CHAPTER THIRTY-FOUR

I felt the wind in my hair as I scootered down the drive, trees sweeping past in a green blur. The gate swung open as I neared it. I hit the accelerator hard.

About five miles or so later, I let off the gas. *God, what a relief.*

My thoughts turned to Danni Beranski. Little wonder she'd broken things off with Billy Ray. Who'd want Marshall Bower for a father-in-law, let alone sweet Georgia Lee as mother-in-law? And Junior? Could he have made a pass at her? Not hard to imagine.

Now, with Lisa pregnant, I could just picture Thanksgiving. Georgia Lee drunk off her ass, Lisa not far behind, Bower Sr., carving the turkey and spouting platitudes, Junior in the bathroom jerking off between doing lines of coke. Lisa's brat (or two or three) running around, wreaking havoc. Straight out of Norman Rockwell.

I aimed the scooter toward Berlin and Danni Beranksi. I had a few follow-up questions.

φφφ

By the time I eased the scooter to the curb before Danni's old Victorian and marched up the steps, it was nearly 3:30. Where had the day gone? I rang the doorbell. No answer. After a minute, I tried again. The chime rang faintly and faded out. No answer. The trees made shushing noises in the yard behind me, as if the bell had disturbed them. Their limbs creaked like those of arthritic elders.

"Sorry," I said, aloud, smiling at my own silly thought.

I opened the screen door and knocked. I was pondering how people always knock after ringing the doorbell—like: *answer now or I'll pound your door down*—when someone behind me said, "Looking for me?"

I jumped and turned. Danni stood there, a shoulder bag slung diagonally across her chest. She held a plastic shopping bag in one hand.

"Sorry," she said. "Didn't mean to startle you."

"That's okay."

"You look a bit pale."

"No, no. I'm naturally pale." And short of breath.

Danni invited me in and offered me water, iced tea, or lemonade. I went for the lemonade, which was fresh squeezed. Boy, was it good. She also helped herself to a glass.

We returned to the porch with our drinks. I took the rocker I remembered, and she took the porch swing again.

"Danni," I said. "Tell me about Junior. Also, anything you recall about Marshall Bower, Sr., and his family."

"Oh, my God!" She looked like she'd just sucked hydrochloric acid. "Just thinking about those people makes me sick."

"Yeah. I can understand."

"Horrible. They were all horrible."

"Did Junior ever, um, come on to you?"

"Good God, when did he ever *not* come on to me?"

Danni poured forth a long narrative about how every dinner at the House of Bower turned into an endurance test, in which she was required to fend off the under-the-table or in-the-other-room advances of her would-be brother-in-law.

"You'd think the guy was on a steady diet of Viagra and porn, the way he kept after me," Danni said. "Jesus!"

"Uh huh."

"I mean, I'd come out of the bathroom, and he'd ambush me and start humping my leg like a dog. You have no idea."

"Oh, I think I do."

Danni's eyes grew large. "No *way* was I going to marry into that family."

Smart girl.

"So, what can you tell me about Marsha?" I asked.

Danni blinked a few times. "Marsha?" Frowning slightly, she stared into her glass. "I hear she was the only decent one in the bunch. But she disappeared."

"Any idea where she might have gone?"

"No," Danni said, "I know she wanted to get as far as she could from … them. Marsha was different. That's all I know."

"Do you think Marsha knew anything about how her father or Billy Ray ran the poultry business? About the working conditions or hiring practices?"

Danni shook her head. "Bower only recently started that business. Marsha's been gone for ages. Long before they got into it. Anyhow, I doubt she'd want to be involved."

Damn it, my leads seem to be drying up!

I spent a bit more quality time with Danni, drinking lemonade, but getting little more than a full bladder to show for the effort. After a quick pit stop, I bid my kind hostess adieu, climbed aboard the scooter and hit the road. *Now what?*

My cell phone vibrated in my pocket. I pulled over and checked the number. Mulrooney. Good news? A dismissal? Hope springs eternal.

I answered. "Mr. Mulrooney?"

"Good day, Sam McRae."

I might have been more charmed by the rhyming bit, if his voice hadn't been a little too happy.

"Is there a reason you're calling? Other than to talk in rhyme?"

"Ah!" The exclamation came out like the climax of an aria. "Yes, I have good news and bad."

"And that would be ... ?"

"The quote-unquote good news is that the state has been processing the evidence in this case quite expeditiously. So they're providing discovery faster than a speeding bullet, so to speak."

"Um, what?

"They're not dragging their feet. They're prosecuting with all due speed."

"Okay." *Which meant the bad news was ...*

"That means things are moving quicker than expected. The preliminary hearing has been moved up to next week."

"Holy shit!" The words slipped out. "You must be kidding? Can we get a continuance?"

"We can try and, of course, we have grounds in our favor. However, you can't assume they'll grant our motion, even if it's a slam dunk." Mulrooney's aria-like tone soured into a dirge. "Frankly, I suspect Bower's attorneys have been maneuvering behind the scenes. Unfortunately, some people feel no compunction about breaking the rules when it comes to making *ex parte* contacts with judges or their staff."

I burned with silent anger. Thanks to these assholes, my friend was looking at going down for a murder she didn't commit. Her presentation on ethics would've fallen on deaf ears among that bunch.

Mulrooney blew an audible breath. "I've told Conroy and I'm telling you, we need to be prepared. And soon."

φφφ

As I finished up with Mulrooney and closed the phone, I felt the brief sensation of the earth falling away. As if its rotation were taking place and I were standing still. Ridiculous. The thought made me dizzy. My surroundings spun. Was it something in the lemonade? Was I simply hungry? Stressed out? Probably just the last two. Honestly, Sam, don't be paranoid.

Focus, I thought. I closed my eyes and took a deep breath. In and out. In and out. Focus and relax. Don't freak out. You'll find the solution. It's probably right in front of your face.

After several minutes of deep breathing my way to relaxation, the world stopped spinning. I boarded the scooter and motored to a nearby sandwich shop to grab a late lunch of meatball sub and onion rings. Greasy, but I deserved it.

What now? Who would have a motive to kill Billy Ray? If it wasn't the terrific trio handling his shady business affairs, then who? What about Marsha? She stood to gain financially. But she'd walked away from her family long before the business even existed and already had plenty of trust fund money. So what would her motive be?

While I scarfed down my food, I thumbed through the issue of *Poultry Today*, which I'd snagged from Bower's office. It was among the effects in Jamila's car that I'd moved into the storage compartment of the rented scooter. I hunted through it now, in a desperate bid for information of any sort. My gaze caught on an item at the bottom of the "Chicken Feed" gossip column, which read:

> A benefit concert for Sea Turtle Saviors will be held in San Diego, CA on July 31, 2006. The Costa Rica-based nonprofit is believed to have been established by an individual or entity connected with the poultry industry.

Something clicked.
Big operations south of the border.
And Maria Benitez.
Bingo!

CHAPTER THIRTY-FIVE

Okay, I had a theory. Maria Benitez could be saving sea turtles in Costa Rica. Or not. This led to all sorts of interesting possibilities, if you applied the "follow the money" principle.

Suppose Maria Benitez was involved in the business, but not directly. Maybe she was using the nonprofit as a front. And Maria was probably more than just Dwayne's drug supplier. She no doubt supplied illegal help to Curtis. Labor in Central America is so much cheaper and good help so much more plentiful than here. Plus, the nonprofit could be used to launder money. How convenient.

Right now, all I had was a name and a theory. One problem: how to prove it, by next week? Or, better yet, in the next two days?

Meanwhile, I wondered if Jamila had been scratched from the program yet. And I still owed Jinx Henderson an answer to her question about Ray.

Damn it, what do I do? I stared at the greasy remains of my onion rings. I had no access to the necessary databases to confirm anything. Conroy would tell me to buzz off, in less polite words. How could I find the help I needed stranded here on these alien shores?

Then, I realized, *Sam, you're an idiot!*

I retrieved my cell and speed dialed the number.

As it rang, I muttered, "Pick up. Please pick up."

Then, I heard, "Reed Duvall."

"Oh, thank God!"

"Well, that's a first." Pride or triumph underscored his tone.

My face grew warm. "Um, that wasn't exactly …"

"Sam, what can I do for you?" Duvall sounded his normal self again. Maybe slightly playful.

"Got an urgent assignment for you."

"Aren't you at the beach? Attending some convention?"

I sighed. "Yeah, but things got, um, a bit complicated. Got a few minutes?"

"Sure thing. Shoot."

Reed Duvall was a private investigator I'd come to know while working opposite sides of an old case. I ran through the events of the past few days and then asked him to try to confirm that some chick named Maria Benitez was the linchpin in an illegal drug and human smuggling operation. I explained my theory that someone connected with the big operation had killed Billy Ray and framed Jamila. I hoped to nail down my theory by having him confirm a few facts.

When I'd finished, Duvall blew out an audible breath. "When do you need this?"

"Yesterday. Preferably the day before."

He chuckled. "My time machine broke, but I'll get right on this."

"Duvall, I really …" I got choked up and couldn't continue.

"That's okay. We met because of Jamila. Remember?"

I thought back to that case. It was only last summer. Despite working opposite sides, we'd formed a bond. Now we were friends. Or were we more?

"Thanks. Really." I managed to get the words out.

"I will always have your back. I'll call you tomorrow."

"One more thing," I said, before he could hang up. "Could you do a background check on someone named Marsha Bower?"

Duvall repeated the spelling of Marsha's name and her last known address as he took the information down.

"She's disappeared," I said. "No one has a clue where she's gone."

"I'll see what I can find," Duvall said. "I'll check for death records and so on, as well as any recent address listings."

As I disconnected, I nearly wept with joy.

Wolfing down the last bite of meatball sub, I gathered the trash and threw it out. By now, it was after 5:00. I decided to test my latest theory of the case on the witness who fingered Jamila in the lineup. I left the sub shop, hopped on the scooter, and sped off to Bayview Drive.

φφφ

I returned to Roger Powers's tidy rancher. In the early evening light, it looked charming, tucked between two others with the bay's grayish-blue waters glimmering in the background. A one-car garage and a healthy rectangle of lawn made his house a standout. I pulled into the asphalt driveway and left the scooter near the garage. Powers must have seen me coming, because he opened the door before I'd gotten halfway up the walk.

"Hi," he said, ambling out.

"Hi, remember me?" We shook hands. The corners of his mouth turned down.

"I'm not sure I'm supposed to talk to you."

"Look, I'm not here to twist your arm. I'm only here to find out the truth."

My words were meant to reassure Powers, but he looked almost frightened.

He said nothing. Gulls cried and kids on WaveRunners motored about on the water, laughing and squealing. Powers and I stared at each other.

"I just wanted to review a few small points, okay? Let's start with something easy," I said. "Did you get a close look at my client?"

"Well, of course."

"In the dark?"

Powers grunted assent.

"So you're sure it was her?"

"Absolutely."

"And you don't wear glasses?"

"No."

"Were the porch lights on?"

"I … can't recall."

Uncertainty. Good.

"But you're sure it was my client, even though it was dark. And my client is dark skinned. So she'd be, frankly, difficult to see."

Powers shifted from foot to foot. "I know what I saw. Why would I lie?"

Good question.

I looked straight into his eyes and asked, "What were you doing out that night when you saw my client at the murder scene?"

"I told you. I was on my bicycle coming home from work."

"Ah. So … where do you work?"

"I told you that, too. I currently have a gig every weekend at the Oceanfront Arms Hotel. It's a new luxury hotel." Powers paled a bit.

"Right. You mentioned that. So … you're a musician?"

"Yes. I play guitar. With a band. Classic rock. Oldies. '80s. '90s. Whatever."

"Okay. Do you own this house?"

"Oh, no. I couldn't afford this. I rent."

"Uh huh. And who pays your band?"

"Well, the Oceanfront management, of course."

"Naturally. Do you happen to know who owns the hotel?"

"How would I? Why would I care?" Powers was sweating. His voice took on a whiny edge.

I patted his arm. "Don't worry about it. I'll find out. And thanks. You've been a great help."

I turned to go, then stopped and looked back.

Powers froze like a statue.

"By the way," I said. "You ever hear of anyone named Maria Benitez?"

Powers' jaw dropped.

"Yeah. That's what I thought," I said. "Thanks for the confirmation."

I marched over to the scooter and mounted it, leaving Powers with his mouth agape and his pants around his proverbial ankles.

CHAPTER THIRTY-SIX

I stopped by the condo to pick up the laptop. Jamila was on the phone. Sounded like she was having a pleasant talk with her auto insurance company about her coverage. As I ducked inside, she said, "Hold on a moment," and set the receiver down with a loud clunk, fixing me with a killer look.

"You would not believe what I've been through today," I told her. I launched into a brief summary of the bizarre events that morning at the Bower residence, followed by the eye-opening discussion with Danni, my phone call with Reed Duvall and my interrogation of the witness who fingered her in the lineup. I skipped over a lot of the gory details about Karla, Dwayne, and Curtis, and didn't speculate about the big operation. I still needed confirmation of a few facts before I told Jamila more. She was my client and had to be treated like any other.

Jamila sat transfixed, her phone call seemingly forgotten. I pointed to the receiver. She blinked several times and picked it up. "Sorry. Can I call you back?" She hung up almost immediately.

I tucked the laptop into its case and made ready to leave. "While Duvall is tracking down the information I want, I'll investigate on my own. First thing, I'm checking out who owns the Oceanfront Arms Hotel. I have a funny feeling about this Roger Powers guy."

"Well, look out for that damn van," Jamila called after me, as I left. "Those journalists have come by twice trying to get an interview since you were last here."

I looped the laptop case strap across my chest like a bandolier and mounted the scooter. I took off, hanging a left on Coastal Highway and keeping a sharp eye out for a coffee shop with free Wi-Fi. Being that it was a late Thursday afternoon in June, early-bird vacationers were making the traffic a bit heavy. This was both a blessing and a curse. With movement slow, I had more time to view my options. I spotted a place within a few blocks. A small bakery tucked away in a strip shopping center, between a bikini store and a shop that sold candles, handcrafted goods, and knickknacks that gather dust and cat hair.

I parked the scooter, went inside and ordered a large black coffee and a big cinnamon roll. I don't care how much cholesterol they have. If I can't eat cinnamon rolls, I don't want to live.

I settled into a corner table. After booting up the laptop and connecting to the Internet, I found the website for Maryland's corporate filings agency, which had a searchable online database. In a separate window, I went to the homepage for the Oceanfront Arms Hotel, which included the notation "MEB Enterprises Inc." at the bottom of the screen. *Gee, I wonder what MEB stands for?*

I entered "MEB Enterprises" into the search box for the agency and hit Return. To no great surprise, it turned out to be a holding company that owned a slew of businesses. Including Bower Farms, Inc.

My thoughts raced. I'm no super genius, but even I could connect these dots. Powers was just a poor musician working at Bower's hotel. Someone saw the opportunity to use him and paid him to be a witness against Jamila. The question was, who? Maria? Powers had reacted at the mere mention of her name. But how would she have known about our confrontation with Billy Ray? This brought me back to the connection between Dwayne Sutterman and Maria Benitez. He could have told her about it. This also raised the question of motive. What would Maria's motive be for killing Billy Ray? Or Curtis? Did he simply represent a loose thread that had to be eliminated? Was he not only a threat to the big operation, but an accomplice to murder? More questions. Hopefully, Duvall could supply a few answers. Preferably by tomorrow.

I drummed my fingers on the table. There's something more, I thought.

Conroy!

I drew in a sharp breath. "That son of a bitch!" Heads turned as I shut down the laptop and stowed it in its case. I finished off my pastry and coffee, picked up the carrying case, and made for the door.

φφφ

I motored back to the condo to return the laptop to safety, repeating countless times the five-word expletive marking my exit from the coffee shop. I had asked myself once before what Conroy had been doing all this time. Clearly, it didn't include doing a simple investigation into the most damaging witness the prosecution had to offer in its case against my client. I caught a distinct whiff of something rotten in the state of Maryland.

Jamila was taking a shower. Good. I had no desire to wait or explain. I left the laptop and hit the road.

I headed back to Coastal Highway, turned north, and pushed the scooter as hard as I could. *If only I'd thought to get the tag number of the silver compact parked outside Conroy's house.* But how could I have known? Even now, I had no proof of anything. Yet.

Traffic was building and slowing to a crawl. Several blocks to go. *Damn.*

If I tried to maneuver between cars, I'd probably get ticketed. Cops were on the lookout at this time of year for violations of that sort. Any sort.

Even so, I thought about it. I checked my mirror. No cop cars. Good.

However, several cars behind me… Was that the beat-up old green Chevy?

CHAPTER THIRTY-SEVEN

I blinked. The cars shifted and the Chevy disappeared from view.

Don't panic, I thought. There are plenty of green Chevys.

I kept an eye out, anyway. As the traffic moved forward, I caught another glimpse of the vehicle. Through the darkened windshield, I made out the silhouettes of two people in the front seat. Were they looking my way? I couldn't see their features.

I took a deep breath. Traffic began to move more freely.

"Quit worrying," I muttered.

I hit the gas and sped toward my destination, glancing at the mirror now and then. The green car receded into the distance but didn't disappear.

By the time I reached Pine Shore Lane, it felt like déjà vu. The setting sun gave the tall condos on the beach a golden hue against the indigo sky. I turned left onto the street and pulled up a few doors down from Conroy's house at 2555. There was his blue Toyota. And there was the silver late-model compact I remembered. Delaware tags. Coincidence?

I set the scooter on its kickstand and strolled over to take a nonchalant look-see.

A sticker in the window showed it was a rental. Interesting. I read the tag number and repeated it as I walked away. Fishing through my shoulder bag, I pulled out my small notepad and pencil and jotted the number down before it evaporated from memory.

I hit the speed dial for Reed Duvall, but cut the call off mid-ring when I saw the green Chevy.

Who the hell are those guys?

I didn't know and I wasn't hanging around to find out.

I jumped on the scooter, started it and took off.

In my mirror, I saw the car execute a three-point turn.

"Shit!"

It wasn't two in the morning. This wasn't going to be easy or fun.

I hit the corner and made a right with barely a glance the other way, squealing tires as I took the turn.

Traffic was heavy. I had to keep my arms steady or risk wiping out. I maneuvered through the vehicles, trying to keep my cool and exercise judgment about my moves. Weaving the scooter back and forth between cars, I managed to hold her steady, like a two-wheeled Mario Andretti.

I stole a quick look in the mirror. The green Chevy was several car lengths behind and bearing down fast.

"Damn it!"

As we approached the downtown area, the same problem as the night before lay ahead: a dead end and turnabout. Edging my way lane by lane to the right, I made a quick turn onto a side street. The green car followed. I cruised west a block or so until I spotted a gap between two buildings. I rolled to a stop and eased the scooter through the narrow opening into an alley on the other side. The green car pulled up near the entrance. I couldn't see inside the tinted window, but I knew the driver must be looking at me. I waved goodbye and motored off.

"Jesus, that was close," I said. I went several blocks down the alley and pulled over. Digging out my cell phone, I hit the speed dial.

"Sorry," Duvall said. "I still don't have all the information for you."

"Don't jump to conclusions. There's something else I need you to check out."

φφφ

After I finished talking to Duvall, I punched the button to disconnect, only to sit and stare at the phone. I needed a car for what I had to do. Should I simply call the closest Avis or Hertz rental office? Should I borrow Jamila's laptop and look for the cheapest deal? I didn't want to borrow her rental and put it at risk.

As I mulled options, I noticed a car heading toward me. A green Chevy, of course. Must have worked its way to the alley through the mazelike side streets.

"Great." I stowed the phone, started the scooter, and burned rubber.

The alley provided a nice traffic-free zone. However, I still had to dodge garbage cans and a moonscape of potholes. Behind me, my pursuer stayed on my tail.

I counted the cross streets down as we approached the Route 50 Bridge. Fourth Street, no cars coming, Third, no cars, Second, a car rolled by just before I reached the intersection. I wove around its rear end and continued straight down the alley.

At First, I hung a sharp right, skidding halfway across the street and barely managing to keep upright. I aimed toward the next street over, but faked them out by taking another alley. They overshot it. While they were backing up and trying to make the turn, I gained distance on them. I cranked the accelerator and took her as fast as I could without wrapping myself around a phone pole. *This is insane, but who are those guys?*

I came to my senses a few blocks later. I backed her down in time to cruise safely into an area where the street ended in a small park with a promenade running alongside the inlet to the bay. The salty breeze blowing off the water was bracing. The gulls cried. Was it in sympathy or mockery? I stopped the scooter and watched them swooping, listened to their cries. I shrugged. “Oh, fuck you,” I said. I started laughing. Hard. So hard it brought tears.

I could hear boats on the water, engines pulsating. Then another sound. One I didn’t want to hear. I looked up. The green Chevy. It had pulled into the lot’s entrance, blocking me in. Shit!

My scooter was idling beneath me. I eased it toward the pavement and over the curb. “See if you can follow me now.” I hit the gas and headed down the promenade.

I could hear car doors slamming behind me. The promenade narrowed behind a building into a thin strip of pavement, a railing separating it from a drop-off onto the rocky shoreline of the inlet. I would have appreciated the water view if I hadn’t been so focused on staying upright and maintaining a decent speed.

I emerged from behind the building into the corner of an overflow parking lot with a hodgepodge of retail stores, restaurants, bait shops, and boat supply and maintenance service providers. Then the pavement simply ran out.

The sky had darkened to slate blue. The sunset was a breathtaking explosion of blood-red, orange, and yellow stripes spread above the clouds. I pondered my next move.

A pair of headlights zeroed in on me. One wall-eyed. The green Chevy.

I hurriedly turned the scooter to go back from where I’d come.

The car chirped to a halt. Two people exited. One called, “Wait!” A woman’s voice.

I looked at her. She waved both hands. "Please. Can I just talk to you?"

"What do you want?"

The woman approached. Her companion, a man, perhaps sensing my apprehension, stood by the car.

As she drew near, I saw she was no older than 25 or so. With shoulder-length blonde hair and dark eyes, she didn't look especially threatening. "Please. Hear me out."

I took a breath and relaxed my shoulders. "You guys need to get your headlight fixed."

"Huh?"

I waved a hand. "Never mind. Why have you been following me?"

She reached into her purse. I started to tense up again. "I'm with the press," she said. She pulled out a wallet and showed me her press pass. I think it was a point of pride. "Barbara Feldman. The Wicomico Weekly Alternative. Ever hear of it?"

"Nope."

"We provide long-form journalism articles. Behind the scenes and in-depth reporting. The kind of thing that mainstream print and broadcast journalism can't handle."

"Uh huh."

She yammered on for a bit about the importance of a free press and how journalism was turning to shit. I nodded.

When she paused, I said, "So, why were you following me? At three o'clock in the morning?"

"Oh, that. I'm sorry. We were up late, putting the paper to bed and we'd stopped to get a drink or two. We ended up closing the bar. We work evenings, so my cameraman, Clint, and I tend to be night owls. We just happened to notice your car and hoped we could talk to you."

"You guys must be desperate for a story, because you scared the living crap out of me," I said.

Barbara's mouth turned down at the corners. Her eyes gleamed with seemingly genuine remorse. "I'm awfully sorry.

It's just that we've tried so many times to reach your client Jamila Williams. She's not answering the door. Or her phone. We were hoping to get her side of the story about what happened to her brother."

I peered at the reporter. "Her brother? Jamila doesn't have a brother. She's an only child."

The reporter fell silent for a moment. "You don't know, do you?"

φφφ

When I returned to the condo, no one was home. I grabbed a book and sat in the easy chair facing away from the front door. Jamila returned 15 minutes later. I heard her storing things in the kitchen behind me. I set the book aside and pondered my next words.

She crumpled a plastic bag, tossed it and walked into the living room. I shifted in the chair and she jumped.

"Sam, for God's sake. I didn't know you were here."

"Hi. I'm sorry. I didn't mean to scare you."

Jamila moved to the sofa and sank onto it. "Well, guess what?"

I smiled at the irony. So much I could say. This wasn't the time for sarcasm. Or twenty questions. "What?"

"I'm probably going to be taken off the program. Big surprise!" She threw her hands out.

"Yeah, speaking of which …"

Jamila hadn't seemed to hear. "Plus my hearing has been moved up to next week. Goody!"

I nodded and murmured, waiting for a break.

She stopped and shook her head. "I'm sorry. This has been the most unbelievable time. Anyway, how was your day?"

I took a breath. "Funny you should ask. For the last few days I've been followed by a couple of reporters. I didn't know they were reporters until today, when they caught up with me. Apparently, they haven't been able to reach you."

Jamila looked hurt and a trifle defensive. "You know as well as I that I'm not supposed to talk to the media."

I paused before answering. "I know that. We need to talk about what the reporter told me about you and your brother."

Jamila's face turned sallow. She worked her mouth, but no words came.

I leaned toward her. "Jamila. Please just tell me what happened to Bobby."

APRIL 1968

CHAPTER THIRTY-EIGHT

It was just another Thursday. Jamila walked home from Salisbury Elementary School with Laura, her second-grade classmate. Laura had raven locks, rosy cheeks, and blue eyes and lived down the street. She had the kind of assets that would come in handy later.

At eight years old, neither of the girls thought about that now. They were too focused on more important things, like *Rowan and Martin's Laugh-In*, *Lost in Space*, Bill Cosby's latest record, the Beatles, and the Monkees.

"My sister gets *Tiger Beat* magazine," Laura said, making it sound like a secret sin.

"I wish I had an older sister." Jamila frowned and felt a stab of envy. All she had was a younger brother. And they barely communicated.

"I can bring the latest issue over tonight." Laura imparted the information with breathless enthusiasm.

Jamila shrugged. "Okay. C'mon by after dinner."

Laura jumped up and down, clapping her hands. "Yippee. See you later."

Jamila watched Laura get smaller as she ran down the street to her house.

Jamila walked in, greeted her mother, and went to her room to do homework. After finishing her homework, she helped with dinner chores—setting the dining room table, stirring the pots, checking the casserole. Her three-year-old brother, Bobby, sat in the living room, watching cartoons. Her father arrived home at quarter to six, looking tired.

"Hard day?" her mother asked.

"You don't know the half of it." Jamila's father tossed his jacket on the sofa and dropped beside it with a grunt. "I'm beginning to think I made a mistake."

"What do you mean?"

Jamila's father shook his head. "Doing legal work for farm workers. It's draining the life from me."

Jamila's mother stopped fussing over the stove and sat beside him on the sofa. Jamila was all ears. Little Bobby's attention didn't stray from the TV.

"What's got you so discouraged?" she said in a soft voice, though Jamila could hear her plain as day.

"It's the people I'm up against. Frankly, racism is endemic to this place."

"Shh. Keep your voice down." Jamila's mother urged, with a quick glance toward Jamila, who feigned indifference.

"I wonder how much longer I can keep this up. How much longer can I fight this system?" He gave Jamila's mother a long look. "I don't want our children growing up in a place where people feel entitled to call them niggers."

"Okay, tell me where they don't."

Jamila felt a twinge of anxiety in her gut. She hated to hear her parents argue or even disagree. It didn't happen often, but when it did, it upset her.

After a bit of back and forth between her parents, Jamila's mother rose and returned to the kitchen. She and Jamila prepared to serve dinner. At shortly after six, Jamila told her father dinner was almost ready. As she returned to the dining table, she saw the cartoon had been interrupted by an announcement. Her father rose to bring Bobby to the dining table. On his way, he raised the TV's volume.

"We interrupt this program to inform you that the Reverend Martin Luther King, Jr., has been shot outside his motel in Memphis, Tennessee. At this time, Reverend King is being taken to the hospital …"

The announcement was interrupted by a crash. Jamila looked at her statue of a mother. The casserole dish and its contents had scattered across the floor, sending ground beef, tomato sauce and noodles everywhere. Amid the shards and food, Jamila's mother remained frozen. Never had Jamila seen such a look of sheer agony and panic on her mother's face.

Turning toward her father, Jamila saw even more despair. What was happening? Who was this Reverend King they were talking about?

Bobby and dinner forgotten, her father walked to the sofa and simply collapsed onto it. "Oh, my God."

φφφ

That night, the television was declared off-limits to Jamila.

"Go to your room and read, sweetheart." Jamila's mother half pleaded her demand.

"What's happening?" Jamila asked. Everyone seemed to be going crazy. The house felt like it was filled with static electricity. One wrong word and a spark would blow them all up.

Jamila's father watched television and kept shaking his head. "I don't believe this." He must have said it a hundred times.

"Laura is supposed to come over," Jamila said.

"No." The vehemence in her mother's voice startled her. "Laura's not coming over." She bit her lip. "Not tonight."

φφφ

Jamila tossed and turned while her parents stayed up late talking. She'd close her eyes and open them, the dim light from the living room leaking under her door. Jamila pounded her pillow and repositioned it several times, but she couldn't sleep.

Meanwhile, her parents' voices would grow louder and then become more hushed. By 1 A.M., Jamila couldn't lie still a minute longer. She rose and crept to her door, opening it slowly. Her parents' words drifted down the hall toward her.

"I don't understand. You owe them nothing." Her mother sounded frantic.

"I'm their attorney," her father said, sounding resigned. "I owe them my allegiance."

"You won't be able to help anyone if you're dead."

Jamila sucked her breath in. Why would her father die? What did this have to do with anything?"

"Honey, I'll be fine."

"I'd ask for that in writing, if I didn't know how little that was worth."

"Sweetheart, listen. The riots are in the cities, not here. We'll be fine."

Riots? Jamila strained to hear more.

"But you know how some of these people think. You deal with it every day. Now, when they see the news, how do you think they're going to treat us? I think we should get the hell out of here."

"Where should we run exactly? We can't simply run away from this. We have to stand our ground. You understand that, don't you?"

"So. Jamila should just go to school tomorrow? Like nothing's happened?"

Her father sighed. "I don't see any reason why she shouldn't."

"Baby." Her mother's voice broke on the word. "You know when it comes to racism, this place can be worse than Mississippi."

"I know. We just have to be strong and show we won't be intimidated."

φφφ

The next morning her mother took Jamila's drowsiness as a sign of illness coming on and ordered her to stay home.

Her father sat at the dining table, looking skeptical. "She'll have to go back eventually."

"I know." Her mother's mouth pressed into a firm line. "Just not today. Give them the weekend to cool down."

Her father nodded. "You're right. That makes sense." He folded the newspaper he'd been reading and tucked it under his arm, before placing his dishes in the sink.

He kissed Jamila atop her head. "Get some rest. And feel better, okay?"

Jamila wanted to tell him the same.

φφφ

After a lunch of chicken soup for her imaginary illness, Jamila and her mother watched a quiz show, while Bobby played with his toy trucks. The phone rang. Her mother sighed and answered it.

A long moment of silence transpired after her greeting. Jamila fixated on remembering the name of one of the Great Lakes. If she knew the answer, someone else would win $50. The panic in her mother's voice disrupted her thoughts and she turned to look.

"So where is he now?" Her mother's brow furrowed and she clutched the phone with both hands. More protracted silence. "Okay. And what's his condition again?"

Jamila's mother tucked the receiver between chin and shoulder, and stretched the coiled cord to its limit, as she gathered her purse and keys.

"Yes, yes. I'll be right there."

She hung up the phone and stared before her.

"Jamila," she said, without looking at her. "I need to go out."

"What's going on?" Jamila asked.

"You're father's … had a little accident. That's all." She continued to avoid eye contact.

"He's hurt?"

"A little, but he'll be okay. It's not serious."

Jamila wasn't convinced.

After arranging to have the next-door neighbor, Mrs. Murphy, come over and watch Bobby and Jamila, her mother said, "Now, honey, I'll be back. Just do as Mrs. Murphy says, okay?"

Jamila wrinkled her nose. "But she stinks." Mrs. Murphy was a gray-haired widow who smelled of old lavender.

"Don't say she stinks," Jamila's mother said, her voice calm, but intent. "It's not polite."

"I didn't say it to her."

"Jamila Williams." Her mother fixed her with an icy stare. "You know what I mean. I've taught you better than that."

Jamila hung her head. "Yes, mom."

When Mrs. Murphy arrived, Jamila's mother squatted beside Jamila and wrapped her arms around her. She could feel her mother's ragged breath in her ear. "I'll be back soon. Don't worry. Your dad will be fine."

Jamila got the distinct impression her mother might be talking to herself.

φφφ

By dinner time, her parents still hadn't come home. Mrs. Murphy fixed a simple supper of macaroni and cheese. Jamila wasn't wild about macaroni and cheese, but it masked Mrs. Murphy's lavender smell.

"I wonder what's taking them so long," Jamila said, fishing for possible explanations. Bobby played with his food.

"Don't worry, sweetheart. I'm sure everything's okay."

The distant look in Mrs. Murphy's gaze told Jamila otherwise.

φφφ

Hours later, her parents still absent, Mrs. Murphy told Jamila she ought to get ready for bed. Jamila balked but did as she was told.

Jamila was in the hazy netherworld between wakefulness and sleep when a squeal roused her fully alert. *What was that noise?*

She crept out of bed and poked her head out in the hall. "Mrs. Murphy?" she said. No reply.

The house seemed too quiet. Then she heard movement. A scuffling sound.

Could it be her parents, at last? She wondered about the squealing noise, however.

She stepped into the hall and crept toward the living room. "Mom? Dad? Mrs. Murphy?"

Her high-pitched voice seemed to be swallowed in the hush descending upon the house.

With each step toward the living room, her heart beat a little faster. Her breathing increased with it.

Jamila reached the end of the hall and peered into the living room. A chill shot through her when she saw the front door open and Mrs. Murphy on the floor, bleeding from her forehead.

Jamila froze. Her breath caught in her throat. A tall dark silhouette of a hooded figure appeared at the door. She scampered into a nearby room and peeked out.

The hooded figure turned to one side, then the other, then strode into the house. He shoved Mrs. Murphy aside with a booted foot. Another hooded figure followed, then another.

Jamila watched in horror, as anonymous hooded people invaded her home.

Then her mind screamed, *Bobby!*

Where was he?

What could she do?

Call someone.

Sounds of ransacking came from the kitchen and living room. Jamila took stock of her situation. She was in Bobby's room—no sign of him. She suppressed a sudden urge to cry. No time for tears. Must get to the phone.

Jamila stole a glance down the hall. The hooded people were apparently too busy looting the other side of the house to check the bedrooms. Her parents' bedroom was only a few feet away. Just a dash down the hall, a quick phone call, then climb out the window and look for Bobby.

She took one last look toward the living room and sprinted toward her parents' bedroom. She shut the door behind her and locked it, then leapt toward the phone.

"Dial zero," she reminded herself. "Ask for the police."

She dialed the number. An operator answered.

"Please help. I need the police. People have broken into my house …"

"Now, now, little girl. Slow down. I'll put you through to the police. Hold on."

Jamila suppressed the urge to scream and waited.

A woman came on the line and Jamila let loose.

"Please send someone to my house. Strange men have broken in. My brother's disappeared. I'm scared."

"Slow down," the woman said. "Try to remain calm. I need to get your address, okay?"

Jamila gritted her teeth and rattled off her address. "Please send someone. Now!"

"Listen. I need you to keep your head, and just tell me what's going on."

Jamila almost cursed. Her mother would've spanked her backside raw if she'd said the word that had come to mind.

"Little girl? Are you still there?" The woman's tinny voice prompted.

"Ye-e-e-s, I'm here," Jamila responded.

"Good. Now stay on the line. Patrol units will be alerted. Now, tell me what's going on?"

"There are strangers in my house. They've knocked out the lady who was watching us for our mom. My brother isn't in his room. I can't find him. I'm worried."

"There there, honey. It'll be okay. Don't worry."

Jamila's thoughts were interrupted by the sound of the doorknob being jiggled.

CHAPTER THIRTY-NINE

Jamila stared at the door with the receiver pressed to her ear.

"Honey, are you there?" The woman said again.

The rattling grew louder. Then it stopped. She heard voices.

"I gotta go." Jamila whispered and hung up. She scrambled off the bed and to the window, thanking God that her family lived in a one-story rambler. The door shuddered as if a heavy weight thrust against it.

Jamila threw the window open and squirmed halfway out before the door flew open and banged against the wall. She fell the rest of the way out and crawled among the bushes to hide.

Lying prone, she raised her head just high enough to check the window. A white-hooded head stuck out from where she'd made her hurried exit. The black eyeholes revealed nothing in the way of identification. The hood could have hidden anyone.

Jamila recalled how her grandma always said the eyes were windows into a person's soul. The hood seemed to rob the person wearing it of his soul.

"Ya see anything?" A man yelled within.

"Nah." The one at the window answered.

"Fuck it. We got the nigger boy. Let's split."

Jamila's mind raced. *Bobby! Oh, no!*

And where are the police?

Jamila crawled out from under the bushes. She couldn't wait for the cavalry.

Making her way to the tool shed in the backyard, Jamila found a screwdriver with a sharp pointed end. She dug around more, came up with her father's Stanley knife and grabbed that, too.

By this time, the hooded gang was filing out to the car. One of them had Bobby slung over one shoulder. Jamila held back in the shadows, until the last minute. As they started up the car, she ran over and took the Stanley to one of the tires. The blowout was like a small explosion.

These guys aren't going anywhere, Jamila thought. Ha!

The gang got out of the car. Jamila turned, dropped the tools and ran for her life.

"Get her," a man yelled.

Jamila's feet pounded the pavement. Thudding behind her grew louder. She spied a fence to her left. Veering sharply, she ran toward it, crouched quickly and sprang up, grabbing the top. She used the force of her momentum to sling herself over the fence. Once over, she let go and landed on her backside.

Jamila made no sound, though her heart felt like it was trying to burst from her chest. Her butt was sore. As if she'd been paddled. Still, she didn't budge.

She could hear the men on the other side trying to find ways to scale the fence. But they were heavier and not as nimble.

"Excuse me." She heard a man's voice. "What are you people doing on my property at this ungodly hour?"

Clearly, the homeowner had discovered the hooded strangers. She heard mumbled exchanges that might have been apologies. Slowly, Jamila got on her hands and knees and crawled to the fence. She peeked out between the wooden slats.

The hooded men were leaving. Jamila breathed a sigh and slumped in relief against the fence.

Jamila tuned out her surroundings. She'd come so close to being caught, it frightened her half to death. Her thoughts wandered briefly toward Bobby, but she shut them out.

After a while, Jamila's head cleared. She managed to stand up and brush herself off. After collecting herself, Jamila circled the house to the front. She started to approach the door, when she saw the flashing blue and red lights. The police! They must have come without sirens. At last! Thank God!

Jamila ran home. Officers were milling about her yard. Her parents were there. They looked frantic.

"Mom! Dad!"

They looked her way. Her mother's face collapsed in grief. "Oh, my baby!"

Her father, his head bandaged and his arm in a sling, looked stricken. "Thank God."

When Jamila reached her parents, she threw her arms around both. Her mother took her and squeezed the air out of her. She started shaking and choking.

"Mommy?"

"Oh, my baby. Oh, my God."

Tears streamed down her mother's face. Her words were a mournful cry.

Jamila looked around. *Where's Bobby?*

She glanced at the car with the flat tire. There was yellow crime scene tape strung around their yard and people in uniform crawling all over the car.

Jamila felt a ball of ice form in her belly.

"Where's Bobby?"

Her mother let out a guttural wail. Tears gushed

JUNE 2006

CHAPTER FORTY

In the cozy condo by the sea, silence fell as I digested Jamila's story. She stared out the glass doors.

I cleared my throat. "The knife?"

Jamila flinched. She nodded once.

I took a steadying breath. Rising, I moved toward her. I crept, as if approaching a feral animal.

The sun had set and the room was cast in shadow. The dock lights glimmered. Jamila's face shone with tears.

I eased beside her and lowered myself onto the sofa.

"If I hadn't dropped the knife," she said. "Bobby would still be alive."

Jamila's voice sounded choked, barely recognizable. I threw my arms around her and hugged her tight.

"No," I said. "You don't know that."

"I shouldn't have cut the tire. I shouldn't have done anything …"

"How could you have known?" I hugged her harder. "You were very brave. You tried to save your brother."

"But look how it turned out. I screwed up. And how could I just run like that? I left him alone. I should have stayed and done something. Protected him."

"You did what you could. You couldn't have fought those men."

"Face it. I screwed up. I've tried so hard to forget. I thought I'd put this all behind me. But it seems like it'll never go away. How have I lived with myself?"

"You have to accept it. You have to forgive yourself."

Jamila turned from the doors toward me. "Have you ever done anything you were so ashamed of you couldn't tell anyone?"

I opened my mouth, but stopped short of telling her. *What would Jamila think if she knew about me and Ray? How would my married friend feel about that?*

"We've all done things we're ashamed of," I said, avoiding the specifics. "We all have to forgive ourselves. We're only human, after all."

I fixed some herbal tea for Jamila and brewed a small pot of coffee for myself. After we'd settled in with our drinks and Jamila had composed herself, every muscle in her body seemed to release at once. Her shoulders slumped as she leaned forward with forearms planted on her thighs and elbows jutted out.

"The local press found out about what happened," Jamila continued. "After that, Bobby's death became a brief local news sensation. Or so I've been told. Fortunately, my parents decided to relocate quickly, so I wouldn't have to deal with the fallout. That's when we moved to the D.C. area and my dad used his connections to get a job with his firm downtown."

Jamila paused, swallowing hard. "They were never able to catch his killers, you know." She shook her head and blinked back more tears. "I couldn't identify any of the hooded people and neither could the neighbor down the street. No one had information or offered to be a witness. The car was stolen from an innocent person. At least, the police found no link between its owner and the people who broke into the house. Mrs. Murphy couldn't recall anything useful. Bobby was restless and couldn't sleep, so she was going to warm up some milk for him. But, first, she decided to go next door and get her knitting or something. Just pop over for a couple of minutes. No time at all. They must have ambushed her. Maybe they would have broken in. Who knows?

"I'm sorry about not telling you. I've been wound tight as a string since this started. When Mulrooney alluded to what happened back then, I realized people can have long memories. They might assume wrongly that what happened gave me an ax to grind. That just made my guilt over the whole thing even worse. Plus the evidence, the whole business with the panel, and now the hearing being moved up."

"Yeah. Listen. About that. I think I'm onto something. Something that could provide a lead on the real killer. Depending on how things pan out."

Jamila looked at me sidewise. "How's that?"

"I'll let you know for sure after I talk to Reed Duvall tomorrow. But I get the funny feeling that there's something fishy about that witness who pegged you in the lineup."

"Why would he pick me if he didn't recognize me?"

I gave Jamila a hard look. "Think. What talks? Everywhere."

Her eyes widened. "Oh, no!"

"Oh, yes."

"But how will you prove it?"

"Don't worry. I'm sure I can … arrange something with the guilty party."

"Who? Bower?"

"No. He wouldn't dirty his hands with this."

"Who then?"

"I have a theory. I'm waiting for confirmation. Hopefully, tomorrow."

"And then?"

"Don't worry about it. The less you know, the better off you are."

φφφ

The following morning, Jamila's mood seemed to have lightened. By the time I woke up, she was brewing coffee.

"Good morning," she said, pouring me a mug, while I retrieved a box of Cheerios from the pantry.

Jamila actually smiled. "Boy, how about this weather, huh?"

I nodded and fixed myself a bowl of cereal as she talked about plans to go shopping.

They say confession is good for the soul. I had no time or inclination for confessions. My soul probably couldn't bear close examination.

"I think I'm going to head up to the discount stores in Delaware," Jamila said. "I know the convention has started, but I don't want to hang out there while these charges are still pending, you know?"

"Absolutely," I said. "Besides, why not take advantage of the lack of sales tax?" That would keep her busy, which was in everyone's best interests. My cell phone rang. The caller ID was as I'd hoped.

I flipped the phone open. "Talk to me, Duvall."

"Well, hello there. Those aren't exactly sweet nothings, but I'll take them."

I inhaled, and slowly blew out my breath. "Why don't we save the cute remarks for later? Just tell me. Whatcha got?"

"On Marsha Bower, I came up empty. I found an old address for her in Santa Fe, New Mexico, but when I called, the landlady said she hadn't lived there in years. She moved out and didn't leave a forwarding address.

"I checked the public records. Her driver's license has expired, but I can't find a death record."

Most odd. Marsha seemed to have vanished into thin air. I wondered if her family had bothered to look for her after she'd taken off. I recalled the weird look I caught in Junior's eyes when I mentioned her name. What was it? Haunted? Fearful? Hopeful? I couldn't put my finger on it.

"Sam?" Duvall said.

"I'm here. Just got distracted. So what else did you learn?"

"Sea Turtle Saviors is a nonprofit based in Costa Rica. Did you know that Costa Rica has a large nonprofit sector? Did you also know that nonprofits down there are rumored to be used quite often for nasty business like money laundering connected with terrorist activity?"

I blinked. "What does this have to do with Maria Benitez?"

"Nothing. I just thought it was interesting."

I huffed. "Can we stick to the relevant facts, please?"

"Patience, counselor. You never know what piece of information might be relevant …"

I tapped my foot and waited, while he rambled on.

"… so, although I couldn't access their corporate records online, I contacted someone who hooked me up. He knew someone—"

"Duvall," I said. "Can we cut to the chase?"

"Okay. Here's the score. I have the name of the person authorized to transact business for the organization. Who happens to be the same person who rented the silver compact car with the Delaware tags."

"Let me guess," I said. "Maria Benitez."

"You're good."

CHAPTER FORTY-ONE

The next morning, armed with the information Duvall had unearthed, I dropped off the scooter and caught a ride with Jamila to the nearest rental car office, where I obtained my own set of wheels. From there, I took the familiar route north, flying by the look-alike strip malls, faux palm trees, all-you-can-eat buffet signs, fake tiki huts, and bamboo fences, one after the other for blocks until I reached the north end where the towering condos fronted the beach.

I took the left onto Pine Shore Lane and spotted Conroy's dark blue Toyota. No sign of the silver compact. Yet.

I cruised past the house, did a three-pointer, and tucked the car behind an outcropping of shrubbery at the end of the quiet street. From there, I had a clear view of the front of Conroy's house. Fortunately, the car I'd rented was nondescript. A gray Taurus, two-door. Nothing special. Not a car that would stand out in a crowd like my classic '67 purple Mustang or Jamila's silver Beemer.

I slouched behind the wheel and waited, keeping the ignition on and the radio low. Looking for the compact with the Delaware tags.

Time crept by. I checked my watch. A half hour. Nothing. Gulls swooped overhead. A man on the radio sang a catchy tune about being cold but still there. I bobbed my head in rhythm to the music and tapped the wheel with both hands, keeping my eyes glued to the house. A commercial break, followed by another song. Duran Duran singing "Hungry Like the Wolf."

"Got that right," I muttered. "I was cold, but I'm still here. And I'm hungry like the wolf."

I checked my watch. An hour had crawled by. Wait, I thought. Early still. Only 11:00 in the morning.

Cars came and went from other houses on the street. Conroy's place remained eerily silent. Was anyone even home? Was I watching an empty house? It would figure. Checking my watch again, I noted it was coming up on noon.

Should I knock on the door? I rejected the thought. I wanted to see Conroy's visitor before I told him anything about what I knew.

I cranked the engine and considered my next move. Then, he appeared. Conroy emerged from the house and scurried to his car. He ducked behind the wheel, yanked the door shut, started up, and took off like a bat out of hell.

Didn't take a lot of guesswork to figure out my next move. I slammed the car into gear and took off after him.

Conroy approached the intersection. The light was yellow, but he made a left without hesitating. I stomped on the gas, praying the light would hold. When it turned red, I changed strategy and made a right, doing the most perfunctory stop-and-look in the history of driving. Then I swerved left to the first median break to make a U-turn and try to catch up with Conroy.

My foot to the floor, I zoomed in and out of traffic like a maniac, pushing the Taurus to its four-cylinder limit. The engine whined like a hungry toddler. I looked ahead and strained to make out the dark blue Toyota from the pack. I thought I caught a glimpse. I changed lanes quickly. A horn honked.

"Sorry!" I waved an apology to the driver behind me. He gave me the finger. I shrugged. I'd tried.

Again, I scanned ahead. This time, I could clearly make out the dark blue car barreling up the highway toward the Delaware border. I kept him in my sights, making sure to keep several car lengths between us to avoid being detected.

"You're not getting away, you son of a bitch," I murmured.

φφφ

Conroy didn't slow until he'd crossed the state line. A few thousand yards into Fenwick, he made a right into the parking lot for a complex of stilted beach houses. I pulled in and backed the car into a space behind a tall set of cattails in front of the development. I got out, locked the car, and crept up the driveway.

A large, freestanding square brick edifice with gold letters announcing "Fenwick Dreams" stood several feet from me. Conroy was parked at the first building past the entrance, two spaces away from the silver compact. He'd left the car and was already on his way upstairs.

My stomach felt hollow and my throat tightened. I scuttled to the huge brick signage and hid behind it, peeking out to see who Conroy was meeting.

He knocked on the door and waited. When it opened, a woman appeared.

She was tall, slender, brunette, and dark-complected. About Jamila's build, I would have wagered.

Before Conroy could say a thing, she spoke with animation, punctuating her words with thrusts of her hands. Finally, she invited him inside. But not before I snapped a few photos with my cell phone.

"Gotcha!" I said.

φφφ

Conroy emerged about a half hour later, looking none too happy. He trudged downstairs to his car, got in, started it and was on his way out, when I pulled out and blocked his exit.

Conroy honked the horn and looked annoyed. I unfolded myself from the car and gave him a shit-eating grin.

"Hi," I said. "Fancy meeting you here."

Conroy's expression melted. There's no other word for it. He went from annoyed to astonished in less than five seconds.

"I think we need to talk," I said. "Care to join me for a cup of coffee?"

φφφ

After meeting at a coffee shop down the road and ordering a couple of cups of dark roast, we found a corner table where we could talk in private.

"Here's how it's going to work," I said. "I know what you did. I know who you've really been working for. I know, for instance, about the witness who fingered Jamila."

Conroy waved a hand. "I didn't. It wasn't—"

"It doesn't matter. It won't look good, will it? No matter whose idea it was. Because you did nothing to stop it." I stared into Conroy's eyes. "Including telling Mulrooney, right?"

Conroy hung his head. "True."

"Okay. So, in order for me not to blow the whistle on you, and have your PI license revoked, and make you an accessory to first-degree murder after the fact … you're going to do me a favor. Got that, old man?"

CHAPTER FORTY-TWO

After Conroy and I finished our talk, I got on the phone.

"Hey, Jinx," I said.

"Well, have you decided?"

"I'm fine, thank you. And, yes, I think I've decided."

"Oh, good! So will you support me?" True to form, Jinx ignored my little joke at her expense.

"Actually, before I answer, could we meet? I just have one or two more questions for you."

"Questions?" Jinx sounded appalled.

"You did say you'd provide reassurance you'd keep your end of the bargain. I'd like to see some proof of that, before I agree to anything."

Jinx sputtered. "Well, of course. I can arrange that."

"So … can we meet? At your place, perhaps?"

"No, no. How about that coffee place? Java on the Beach?"

Another round of parry and thrust with Jinx in a tiny dump that smelled like rotten fish? Thank God, it wouldn't come to that.

An hour later, I stood outside Java on the Beach. The air was fresher and I knew this wouldn't take long.

Jinx strolled up, looking dapper in khaki pants and a conservative navy blazer over a white shell. Based on her outfit, I assumed she must have been attending the conference. Looking at her made me feel like a kid playing hooky.

"Shall we go in?" she said.

"That won't be necessary," I said, raising my hand, palm out. "I'm saying no to your deal."

Jinx's eyes nearly popped from her skull. "What?"

"I said—"

"I heard you the first time," Jinx snapped. She gazed at me with a wounded expression.

"I'm sorry, but that's my answer."

"You realize I'm going ahead with this? With or without your help?"

I shrugged. "Qué será será. Whatever. So long and good luck with that." I walked away.

"So why the hell did you want to meet?" Jinx called after me.

I stopped and turned to look at her. "I just had to see your face when I gave you the news."

φφφ

Having dispensed with that, I made a few phone calls and stops on my way back up Coastal Highway. I crossed the line into Delaware and turned into the "Fenwick Dreams" complex. I pulled up to the first building past the big brick sign with the gold lettering and parked the car. The silver compact appeared not to have moved.

She was up there. I surveyed the lot. Quite a few cars, actually. Not like we were all alone. Even so, I wondered if this was the ideal place to confront a murderer.

"Silly," I murmured. "You're covered, right?" I had my mace, my wits, my cell phone. And my ace in the hole. Plus

I'd made arrangements. I only hoped I'd been taken seriously.

However, these killers were wily. They'd already killed one person to protect their illegal activities and their culpability as Billy Ray's murderers.

On the other hand, how else was I going to flush them out? To do that, I had to show my cards and let them make a move. I had to do something to keep Jamila from going down for a crime she didn't commit. I simply wouldn't allow it. I couldn't allow it.

I sighed. "Well, Sam. You're not going to accomplish anything sitting here, are you?"

I exited the car and locked up. I climbed the steps to the house Conroy had visited only hours earlier. I rapped on the door.

The elevated beach house afforded a stellar ocean view, which I was admiring when she answered. Tall and slender, she wore a dark tan and a puzzled expression.

"Can I help you?" she asked.

"Hi, Maria," I said. "Or should I say, Marsha?"

CHAPTER FORTY-THREE

The woman gawked at me. "What are you talking about? Who are you?"

"Cut the crap, Marsha. You know who I am. I know who you are. Let's get real, okay?"

The woman crossed her arms and tilted her head back. "I have nothing to say to you."

"Okay, fine." I got up in her face. "We can play it your way. It won't go easy, but once I turn Conroy in to the cops, do you think he won't spill the beans on you? He'll be on his knees begging for a plea bargain. And do you suppose part of that plea bargain will involve turning state's witness against the people who paid him to look the other way while they bribed a witness in a first-degree murder case? Yeah, I'd take that bet—"

"Hey, sis, what's going on?" The voice from within was familiar and unmistakable.

Marsha looked about ready to spit nails.

"Oh, sis," I said. "You want to tell Junior what's going on?"

She said nothing, but pure hatred radiated from every pore.

"What do you want?" she said, finally.

"You have to turn yourself in."

"Fat chance."

"Really? We'll see."

"You gonna make me?"

"I think I can."

"I'd like to see you try."

Our voices must have carried, because who should appear at Marsha's side, but Mr. Horny Cokehead himself.

"Girls, girls … please," he said, grinning and stumbling. "No fighting. Okay?"

He leaned on Marsha's shoulder and raised his glance toward me. The grin vanished.

Marsha turned toward Junior and glared at him. "Junior, go back to your room. Now!"

Junior turned around and slumped off.

"That's right, Junior. Do what mother says," I goaded. "You know, you might want to keep your brother on a leash. The last time I saw him, he tried to hump my leg."

"Fuck you!" Marsha turned her wrath upon me. "Who are you to judge? How would you feel if your own father gave your birthright to someone else's kid?"

"I haven't the slightest idea."

"No shit you don't." Marsha looked at me with disdain. "Our mother dies and he goes and marries some piece of trailer trash. Then her kid gets to own the family business? Well, the hell with that. I wasn't going to let that happen. That business should go to Junior. Billy Ray was an interloper, plain and simple."

"Interloper. That's quite a word. So many syllables. Almost as many as in premeditated. As in first-degree murder. I'm so disappointed, Marsha. Everyone says such nice things about you."

"Well, I care about my brother. I'm the only one really looking after his interests."

"You care so much, you took your trust fund money and left him high and dry."

"Don't preach to me, honey. I had to live in that house, not you. Once our mother died and our father hooked up with that whore, I simply couldn't stand it."

"Must have been pretty horrible to drive you to leave the country and assume a new name."

"You can't prove any of that."

"Oh, but Conroy knows all about it. I'm sure he'll be more than willing to share what he knows to keep his ass out of prison. Not to mention having his private eye license yanked and his reputation turned to shit."

Marsha closed her eyes and lifted a hand to her brow, rubbing it. A tear formed in the corner of one eye.

"I only wanted to help Junior. I swear."

"It's over, Marsha. One way or the other, the truth will come out. Now, you can either admit what you did or sully Conroy's reputation by forcing him into a plea bargain in which he turns state's witness against you. Do you want that on your conscience, too?"

Marsha paused, as if considering taking a dive off a cliff. The moment stretched to eternity. Her answer would make or break my deal with Conroy.

I wasn't looking to bring Conroy down. Who was I to judge the man? But Marsha had to confess her mortal sins if I hoped to make an airtight case for Jamila's innocence.

Finally, Marsha exhaled. "Okay, fine. I kept in touch with Dwayne and Curtis after I left Maryland. They kept tabs on Junior and let him know I was okay, without giving away too much detail."

"Were you using the nonprofit as a front for laundering money from drug smuggling and bringing illegal aliens into the country?"

"I don't want to talk about that."

I can just imagine.

"My point," she continued, "was that they kept me apprised of events. Every now and then, I come into town on business and stay here incognito. When I heard that vicious slut Lisa Fennimore had sunk her greedy little hooks into my brother, I came here. I told Junior he should insist on an amnio before he marries that gold digger. I'll bet anything that's not even his kid."

"So, you think Lisa hopes to get her hands on the business, too?"

"Lisa just needs to get married to access her trust fund. She doesn't give a damn about my brother or the business. And my father obviously gave up on Junior ages ago. That rat bastard!"

I nodded. "Did you come to Maryland intending to kill Billy Ray?"

Marsha shook her head, looking glum. "No. It's just that … after I heard what happened in the parking lot, I sensed an opportunity to get rid of the guy for good, and keep free and clear of the whole mess. But, I swear to God, all I wanted was to get that scum sucking man out of our lives. I killed him to protect Junior."

"Except, of course, if your father dies, you're the one who inherits the business now, aren't you?"

Marsha paled. She raised a hand to her chest and sputtered. "I didn't kill him for my gain. I swear, I did it for Junior. I'm going to take care of him."

"Like you took care of Curtis?"

Marsha shook her head. "You don't understand. Dwayne said Curtis was jeopardizing our whole operation. We had to get rid of him."

"Who? You and Dwayne?"

"I … I'm not saying anything more." She crossed her arms.

Far as I was concerned, that was as good as an admission. With any luck, the cops could tease out the details. I turned and scanned the distance. "Here they come."

Marsha's mouth was agape. "Who?"

"The cops. They're here."

I waved a hand toward the cop cars pulling into the driveway.

"Why? How?" Marcia asked.

"I told them my theory. And now you've confirmed it." I opened my shoulder bag and revealed the small tape recorder I'd borrowed from Barbara Feldman of the Wicomico Weekly Alternative. She'd have a big scoop on her hands now.

"Marsha," I added. "Just so you know, I didn't have a birthright. My parents both died when I was nine. And sometimes life just isn't fair."

CHAPTER FORTY-FOUR

That evening, Mulrooney was in his cups. Based on the taped confession, the cops were willing to drop the charges against Jamila. After the cops had taken Marsha and Junior in, he'd used his not inconsiderable influence to set up a quick hearing and get the charges against Jamila dismissed that afternoon.

Fortunately, the recording was obtained without police knowledge, thus negating Fourth Amendment concerns. Admissible or not, it provided plenty of probable cause to arrest Marsha and Junior. The siblings had lawyered up, but the recording had already done significant damage.

Mulrooney had even managed to wangle two additional days free stay for us at the condo from Bower, Sr. In exchange, Mulrooney provided every assurance that he'd keep the big man's name out of it when he spoke to the press about the matter. Clearly, Bower, Sr. was pulling out all the stops to distance himself from the actions of his wayward kids.

I called Russell to let him know I'd be taking a couple more days off. Any concern I had that he might feel put upon melted away when he said, "Good for you. Take another week, if you like."

"Well, that's not necessary," I said. "But thanks for offering."

"Having fun?" Russell's nasal voice intoned.

"Yeah, I'm having a blast." I was so not going there. "How's Oscar?"

"The little asshole?" I could picture Russell, in his smoking jacket, with scotch on the rocks in hand. "He's just fine. You know I'd call you if there was a problem, right? Now, have fun and don't worry about a thing."

I tried to swallow the lump forming in my throat. "Thanks, Russell." *I love you, too.*

φφφ

The three of us celebrated with dinner at one of Mulrooney's favorite seafood restaurants. The Crusty Claw was right by the bay and had piers, making it accessible by car or boat. Seated at a table on the outdoor deck, we toasted our success with a bottle of Chardonnay and watched the sun melt into the clouds, spreading its dying glow like hot butter.

When the waitress, a petite blonde who looked about sixteen, took our order, I couldn't help but notice her slight foreign accent.

I smiled and said, "I take it you're not from around here?"

She shook her head and returned the smile. "I'm from Germany. However, for the next few years, I'll be attending Oxford."

I nodded. That was one foreigner with a temporary visa who wasn't going to be picking crabs or hauling chickens to slaughter.

Naturally, Jamila was in high spirits. "I'm so relieved this is settled. And I'm on the program tomorrow. No question."

"I'm glad we could make the whole thing go away," I said.

Jamila looked at me. For a moment, I thought she looked sad.

I smiled. "It's over, Jamila. Everything's fine. You're in the clear."

She beamed. "Of course." She leaned toward me and squeezed my arm. "And I have you to thank for that."

Our food arrived around the time they lit the tiki torches. The water shimmered inky dark with silver glimmers of reflected moonlight and squiggly yellowish-white streaks cast off from houses and dock lights along the shore. Boats with green and red lights eased by now and then, creating the illusion of illuminated dots skimming over the water.

Mulrooney had opted for all-you-can-eat steamed hardshell crabs. Jamila chose crab cakes. I dined like royalty on flounder stuffed with crab imperial.

"Thanks again for taking us out, Mr. Mulrooney," Jamila said. I kept picking at the crab, expecting to find shells and cartilage, but it had neither.

I avoided thoughts of Luisa and her kids working side by side to keep my dinner free from annoying bits of inedible matter.

Mulrooney attacked a blue crab with a knife, wedging it in the crack between the shells. "Think nothing of it. Frankly, I'm glad Sam and Conroy were able to find out what they did, so we could get the matter dropped before the state began prosecution proceedings."

"Yeah." I glanced at Jamila, who was working on her salad. She didn't know a thing.

"Thank your lucky stars you're not defending the case now," Mulrooney continued, deftly flipping the crab shell apart. "The feds are crawling all over it. The INS, the DEA, the IRS. You name it. It seems Marsha was quite the entrepreneur. The nonprofit was saving sea turtles, but it was also allegedly engaged in various illegal activities, including money laundering."

I smiled. "I just love cases involving the feds," I said, clearly not meaning it. This reminded me a bit too much of a previous case involving people who changed their identities, committed crimes, and attracted feds like flies to chicken shit.

"You have to admit, Marsha is a pretty shrewd business woman," Mulrooney said.

"That's one way of putting it," Jamila said. "Criminal queenpin is another."

I chuckled but thought back to my talk with Danni. She said Marsha wanted to be different from her family. But how far had the apple really fallen from the tree?

"My theory is Marsha and Dwayne killed Curtis," I said. "Were the police able to apprehend Dwayne?"

Mulrooney nodded. "The idiot was found this afternoon. His boat nearly reached Chincoteague before it ran aground. On alert by the local police, the Coast Guard arrested him and impounded the boat."

Hmm, I thought. Marsha would no doubt want to trade information in order to plea to a lesser charge than first-degree murder and since she was a member of the influential Bower clan, I suspected Dwayne was royally screwed.

"So … I wonder who called me from Curtis's phone?"

Mulrooney gouged crab meat from the shell. "Marsha."

"Why?"

"According to the police, Curtis was already dead. Marsha admitted to making the call to throw them off and make you a suspect, too."

"You're kidding."

"It worked. Marsha's a pragmatist."

"That's one word for it," I said.

CHAPTER FORTY-FIVE

I hate banquets. I hate any occasion that requires wearing a dress. Lately, when I go to court, I've been getting by with pantsuits, depending on whether the judge is able to handle such a radical concept. I'd managed to scrape up a decent form-fitting navy knit number that ended a few inches above the knee.

I checked myself in the mirror, adjusted one leg of my tights and swore. "We should be having fun, not going to some stuffy-ass banquet," I muttered.

"Are you ready?" Jamila appeared at the door, dressed to the nines in a shiny black sequined sheath with a bolero jacket.

"I hate tights. My legs feel like sausages." I struggled with the hose, twisting and pulling. After a final yank, I said, "Fine. I'm ready."

"Aren't you going put on makeup?"

I waved a hand and made a "pfft" sound between puckered lips. "Why? Who am I trying to impress?"

"C'mon, Sam. It's a banquet."

"Exactly. It's a banquet. Not my coming-out party."

As we hustled to grab our bags and get to the car, I thought about those words. "Coming out" took on an interesting possible meaning in light of what Jinx had threatened. However, it would be fascinating to see what the night would actually bring.

"I still can't believe this nightmare is over," Jamila said, as she drove. "I can't believe that woman went to such lengths to set me up."

"It was opportunistic. Since Dad owns the place, Junior was able to get a copy of the key to the condo and slip it to Marsha. So, while we were out on our nature hike on Assateague, she snuck in and stole the knife and clothes."

"All because they knew about our argument the day before?"

"That and the noise complaint that started everything."

"Well, I guess there's a lesson in this, isn't there? If your neighbors make noise, ignore them." She laughed, which made me even happier than I'd felt during dinner the night before.

φφφ

The banquet was standard fare. A big room jammed with round tables hidden beneath white tablecloths, each set for eight people. A long dais ran along the far wall with a head table for the bigwigs. People in their finery milling about, drinks in hand, sampling from a selection of hors d'oeuvres like bacon-wrapped scallops, chicken wings, and mini crab cakes set up over steam trays, plus a big bowl of chilled shrimp on ice with a ceramic cup of cocktail sauce jammed in the middle. The crowd jostled me. The air was stuffy, even though the AC was blasting. Conflicting scents of excess cologne made me sneeze. As is usual at these things, everyone seemed to be talking at once.

While Jamila grabbed a couple of seats at a table near the dais, I got a glass of wine at the open bar. My second glass of wine in two days? I'm not usually a drinker, but this wasn't just any old night. Although I normally would have preferred a table along the periphery, tonight I wanted a front row seat for what I anticipated could be a most interesting show.

As I took my seat next to Jamila, I saw him. Ray was seated at the head table. *Of course.* His very young fiancée, Amy, was next to him. Both of them were beaming. Ray was talking a mile a minute to a gray-haired guy in an expensive navy suit. Clearly, Ray was in his element. He stopped talking and did a visual sweep of the room. His glance drifted my way momentarily, paused a second, and kept going.

"Hey, guys!" Kait Farrell's voice interrupted my thoughts. She walked up to the table and, over her glasses, bestowed a mock glare my way. "Where've you been all weekend?"

"Um, kind of busy." I glanced at Jamila. As always, her expression was unruffled.

Kait made a loud "tsk, tsk" sound, while shaking her head. She smiled at Jamila and said, "Your presentation this afternoon was great, by the way."

Jamila nodded, looking serene. "Thank you."

I looked at Jamila. I felt so proud of her. She looked just like a judge should. I could picture her in robes one day.

"Sam."

I knew the voice. I turned to my left to see Jinx wedged between myself and the man sitting next to me.

"Hi," I said. "What's up?"

"I think you know darn well what's up. There's going to be a show after dinner. A slide show with photos you won't want to miss."

"Okay, Jinx. Are you sure you want to do this, though?"

"Positive."

"Well, I can't stop you."

"Nope."

"Have fun."

Jinx flounced off. Kait had left to join the other state's attorneys. White-coated waiters swarmed the tables, depositing plates of chicken, veggies, and rice before everyone. One glance at the chicken and I thought I'd get sick to my stomach. I ordered a second glass of wine.

"Why do they always have to serve chicken at these things?" I said.

"We're on the Eastern Shore, Sam," Jamila said. "And crab cakes were probably too expensive."

I tried—really tried—to saw the chicken breast and eat little pieces. But there's a reason they call these events "rubber chicken dinners." Knowing what I did about the slaughter of chickens and migrant workers didn't make things any easier.

I polished off my salad, rice, and vegetables, poked the chicken, and gulped my wine. I raised the nearly empty glass to flag a waiter down for another. He brought it, and I swallowed what was left before handing him the empty.

The room seemed stuffy and loud, but I felt good. Really good. Relaxed. I had another swallow of wine. I felt it go down and warm my belly. My face went hot. I picked up a program and fanned myself.

"Is it me or is this place hot as hell?" I asked Jamila, poking her arm and raising my voice above the din.

Jamila, who I'd interrupted mid conversation with someone, turned and looked at me. "Well, it's a bit … You look … um, you look kind of …"

I laughed. "What? I look kind of … what?"

Her gaze drifted toward the wine glass in my hand. "How many of those have you had?"

I shrugged. "Who's counting?" I laughed some more. Everything was funny.

"Maybe you've had enough wine."

"Yeah," I said. I looked around at all the lawyers. So many white faces. Then I looked at the waiters. So many black faces. "Maybe I couldn't possibly drink enough."

Jamila placed a hand on my arm. "Is something wrong?"

My head was buzzing. I thought about telling her. Confession was good for the soul, wasn't it? But once the toothpaste was out of the tube …

I started to speak, when a speaker crackled to life on the podium.

"Okay, everyone. While they're serving coffee and dessert, let's bring this meeting to order. Now, before we get underway—"

"Hold it!"

The voice that rang out from the back of the room was Jinx's. She rushed up to the dais, clutching a laptop with a small projector, and whispered something into the emcee's ear. She placed the equipment on the table near the podium and fired it up. The emcee frowned and hovered near, but she elbowed him aside and stepped up to the mic. A hush fell over the room.

"Ladies and gentlemen," Jinx said into the mic. "It is my sad duty to inform you that the president-elect of this organization has engaged in acts of moral turpitude."

"Hmmph," Jamila said. "Who knew she could even use that word in a sentence?"

I smiled and said nothing.

I looked at Ray. His face was stoic, but his eyes showed fear. His gaze locked onto mine.

"I have pictures here that prove my point." Jinx repositioned herself behind the laptop. She inserted a flash drive into it, clicked the mouse a few times and projected an image onto the wall behind the dais. For a moment, you could've heard a pin drop.

Then, the room exploded in laughter.

Jinx turned and looked at the wall. "No!"

It was a huge photo of her on the toilet.

Jinx shut off the computer, scooped everything up and stalked out without a word.

Jamila and I doubled over. Ray laughed harder than anyone else at the head table. He wiped his eyes, looked at me and smiled. I turned away.

"Well," I said. "That was … interesting."

Jamila shook her head. "I'm … lost for words. Anyhow, where were we?"

"Would you excuse me a moment?"

I got up and stumbled through the tables toward the rest rooms. Jinx's stunt had ground proceedings to a halt. The room resonated with talk and laughter, making me even more disoriented. The wine wasn't helping matters. I pulled out my cell phone and punched in a number.

"Yes," he answered.

"Nice work," I said.

"Thanks. It was no big trick. I just followed her from that dive where you met to her motel. While she was out, I planted a hidden camera and got the photo. I had plenty of time to figure out where she stored the photos of you, too. She left her room for several hours so the maid could clean it today. I was able to make the switch before the banquet with no problem. Now, will you honor your word and keep my name out of it?"

"Yes, Ellis. I can call you that, can't I? We are friends now, aren't we?"

"Sure," Conroy said.

"You make it sound so depressing. I'm really nice, once you get to know me." I hung up.

I took a few moments to use the facilities, then managed to find my table again. Jamila looked at me with concern.

"I was beginning to wonder if you'd fallen in." She placed her hand on my arm again. "Okay, before we were so rudely interrupted, I asked if there's anything wrong?"

I looked at my friend. "It's nothing. Really."

ABOUT THE AUTHOR

Debbi Mack has published two other novels in the Sam McRae mystery series: the New York Times ebook bestseller *Identity Crisis*, and the sequel *Least Wanted.* She's also published *Five Uneasy Pieces*, a short story collection that includes her Derringer Award–nominated story "The Right to Remain Silent." Her short stories have appeared in various anthologies and publications, including *Shaken: Stories for Japan*, an anthology created to benefit Japanese tsunami relief efforts.

A former attorney, Debbi has also worked as a journalist, reference librarian, and freelance writer/researcher. She's currently working on a young adult novel, planning Sam's next adventure, and generally mulling over other projects.

CPSIA information can be obtained at www.ICGtesting.com
Printed in the USA
BVOW040513280612

293845BV00002B/1/P